Prom Crashers

How NOT to Spend Your Senior Year
BY CAMERON DOKEY

Royally Jacked
BY NIKI BURNHAM

Ripped at the Seams
BY NANCY KRULIK

Spin Control
BY NIKI BURNHAM

Cupidity
BY CAROLINE GOODE

South Beach Sizzle
BY SUZANNE WEYN AND DIANA GONZALEZ

She's Got the Beat
BY NANCY KRULIK

30 Guys in 30 Days
BY MICOL OSTOW

Animal Attraction
BY JAMIE PONTI

A Novel Idea
BY AIMEE FRIEDMAN

Scary Beautiful
BY NIKI BURNHAM

Getting to Third Date
BY KELLY McCLYMER

Dancing Queen
BY ERIN DOWNING

Major Crush
BY JENNIFER ECHOLS

Do-Over
BY NIKI BURNHAM

Love Undercover
BY JO EDWARDS

Prom Crashers

ERIN DOWNING

Simon Pulse

New York London Toronto Sydney

SIMON PULSE
An imprint of Simon & Schuster Children's Publishing Division
1230 Avenue of the Americas, New York, NY 10020
Copyright © 2007 by Erin Soderberg Downing
All rights reserved, including the right of reproduction in whole or in part in any form.
SIMON PULSE and colophon are registered trademarks of Simon & Schuster, Inc.
Designed by Ann Zeak
The text of this book was set in Garamond 3.
Manufactured in the United States of America
First Simon Pulse edition February 2007
10 9 8 7 6 5 4 3
Library of Congress Control Number 2006928447
ISBN-13: 978-1-4814-2747-0

Prom Crashers

Prom Crashers

ERIN DOWNING

Simon Pulse
New York London Toronto Sydney

SIMON PULSE
An imprint of Simon & Schuster Children's Publishing Division
1230 Avenue of the Americas, New York, NY 10020
Copyright © 2007 by Erin Soderberg Downing
All rights reserved, including the right of reproduction in whole or in part in any form.
SIMON PULSE and colophon are registered trademarks of Simon & Schuster, Inc.
Designed by Ann Zeak
The text of this book was set in Garamond 3.
Manufactured in the United States of America
First Simon Pulse edition February 2007
10 9 8 7 6 5 4 3
Library of Congress Control Number 2006928447
ISBN-13: 978-1-4814-2747-0

For my parents,
who have always supported my adventures
and who taught me that a weird sense of humor
is not optional

Acknowledgments

Thanks to Barb Soderberg (my wonderful, goofy mom), my cute and clever husband, Greg, and superauthor Robin Wasserman for all your help creating and plotting this story in a hurry. Good ideas, guys! Thanks for letting me steal them.

Ginormous thanks also to my editor, Michelle Nagler, whose suggestions, compliments, criticisms, and humor make me love writing—and writing for her, in particular!

Finally, thanks to Duluth, Minnesota—my hometown—and all the amazing people and places there that inspired a lot of these characters and experiences. Very little in this book is based on reality, but some of it sure comes close. But I'll keep those details to myself, thankyouverymuch.

One

Prom was in less than a month, and Emily Bronson still didn't have a date.

No matter how hard she tried, she just couldn't make herself *not* care. It was so unlike her. Homecoming rallies, student council, the one consistently clean table in the lunchroom . . . she didn't get hung up on any of that. But prom—prom was another story.

So Emily was busy doing what she'd done every night for the past several weeks: leaning against the counter at her after-school job, twisting her silky hair into tiny tangles, and daydreaming about—what else?—prom.

Emily worked at the Leaf Lounge, the

tragically unhip "tea lounge" in the mall, almost every school night until nine—as well as weekends—which gave her more than enough time to daydream. The mall wasn't a superfunky boutique mall with trendy shoe shops and retro bags, either. It was just your run-of-the-mill, suburban mall with four Auntie Anne's pretzel outposts and an Abercrombie in both the east and west corridors. In a word, boring.

The Leaf Lounge—less a true "lounge" than the Gap was trendy—didn't have the urban-funk feel of a hip downtown hot spot. The beige and teal walls were adorned with shoulder-high shelving that boasted the complete collection of "Teas of the World" teapots. The Leaf Lounge's owner, Gary, was thrilled that his was one of the ten shops in the United States that sold those teapots. It was his claim to fame.

As such, Gary wanted all his employees to take great pride in their tea expertise. It was already bad enough that Emily had to work there. The thing that made it worse was being forced to wear a name tag that read:

EMILY, TEA CONNOISSEUR
HOW MAY I HELP YOU?

And she had to act like she cared. Emily had been awarded the distinction of "Tea Connoisseur" after completing a three-hour (mandatory) class in proper high tea preparation. The class had been held in the back room of the Leaf Lounge one Sunday morning before the mall opened, and was run by a woman named Meadow.

Meadow had shouted "pinkies on alert!" repeatedly during the session, which had elicited countless snickers from Emily's cousin and co-worker, Charlie. Needless to say, the knowledge Meadow had imparted had been used a total of zero times since the class—there wasn't a lot of demand for fancy high tea in a suburban mall. Their customer base was just *slightly* less classy.

"I divide, you choose," Frank, one of the Leaf Lounge's regulars, called to Emily across the coffee shop's formica countertop, breaking through her don't-have-a-date-for-prom obsessing. He was gesturing to a prepackaged muffin split down the middle on a plate in front of him. He was the only other person in the shop at that moment, and he seemed eager to chat. "Banana walnut, Emmy." Frank insisted on calling Emily "Emmy," and she had never made an effort to correct him. She thought the nickname was kind of cute. Emily slid half the muffin off Frank's napkin and popped a piece in her mouth.

"Tasty as ever," she declared. "Packaged preservatives. Thanks, Frank." Frank was one of the regulars who spent too many hours at the mall and considered the Leaf Lounge's employees among his best friends. He came in every night around six and stayed for exactly fifteen minutes. He always ordered a prepackaged muffin and a cup of coffee and insisted his seventy-year-old waistline couldn't afford eating a full muffin. So he shared his snack with Emily, knowing it would buy him a few minutes of conversation.

"How's school, Emmy?" Frank smiled through a mouthful of gummed-up muffin. "Lots of gentleman callers?"

"Same old story, Frank." He asked the same question every night. Her answer was always the same. "Zero gentlemen and zero callers. In fact, I don't even have a date for prom yet—got any friends you could set me up with?"

Frank beamed. "Back in my day, the boys would have been lined up around the block to sign your dance card. I bet they're all just too shy to ask."

"That's what I keep telling her." Charlie winked as he slid a tray of cookies across the counter. He had been hiding out in the back room for the past hour, smoking clove cigarettes and pretending to do dishes. "I keep offering to take her myself, but I guess I'm not good enough for her."

"Right—that's what it is." Emily nodded. "It couldn't possibly be that you're my cousin. That's not at all sad."

Frank studied Charlie carefully. "How about you, kiddo? You must be quite the lady-killer." Emily and Charlie exchanged a look. "You don't have a date yet?" To anyone under the age of fifty, it was glaringly obvious that Charlie was 100 percent gay. But Frank was of a totally different generation, and the thought never crossed his mind.

"I do okay," Charlie finally responded seriously. "But no—no prom date yet. My fingers are crossed, though, that the girl of my dreams will turn up one of these days and steal my heart."

Emily shot him a look as she stacked cookies in the cookie jar next to the register. Charlie couldn't say anything without dripping sarcasm. It was part of the reason she loved him, and part of the reason she often lovingly loathed him.

Frank sighed, then tumbled gently off his stool. "It's been a pleasure, Emmy. Charles"—he winked at Charlie—"your time will come . . . with the ladies, I mean." He nodded and shuffled toward the door.

"Sweet guy. Totally clueless," Charlie muttered through clenched, smiling teeth. "So, what are we doing now?"

Emily closed the lid of the cookie jar and turned to Charlie. "Bored?"

"Completely and hopelessly. I can't stand this place for one more second. Entertain me."

"It is *so* not my issue that you're bored. Maybe you could serve a customer or two, and your shift wouldn't feel so long?" Emily pushed past her cousin and into the back storage room. Charlie followed her like a lost puppy. "Hey," she said, thinking about what Charlie had just told Frank about prom. "Aren't you going to prom with Marco?"

"Ah, Marco." Charlie sighed. "Don't I wish."

Emily shot him a confused look. "Am I

missing something? Can't you get him to come up for prom?" Marco and Charlie had been dating for almost a year, but things were complicated by the fact that they had been long-distance almost since the day they had met—Marco lived in a suburb of Chicago. Emily could never keep up with the drama.

"He doesn't believe in prom," Charlie stated simply. "He thinks it's an antiquated social custom that should have died with the eighties." He shrugged. "Plus, I'll see him in June when we get to the villa." The words rolled off Charlie's tongue as if spending a summer at an Italian villa was totally normal.

Charlie and his parents spent six weeks every summer in Northern Italy, which is where he and Marco had met the year before. Their romance had been kick-started during four shared weeks in the Italian Alps. Emily could think of nothing more idyllic, and every ounce of her wished that (1) *she* got to spend the summer in the Italian Alps instead of her suburban backyard, and (2) Marco was straight so it could have been *her* fairy tale (in addition to the Italian setting, Marco was hot). But she was happy for her cousin—when she wasn't overcome with jealousy.

"You tell Marco," Emily teased, "that prom is a rite of passage that should be respected. Prom rocks." She furrowed her brow seriously. "Unless I don't find a date, and then prom sucks." She grabbed a big bag of coffee beans off one of the shelves and returned to the front of the store. Charlie was still trailing behind her, hands empty.

"I'm with you," Charlie agreed, hopping up to sit on the counter. "I'm hoping he'll call me one day and tell me he's fully into prom and on his way here, but I think it's a lost cause. I'll find someone to go with—I can't say I'm worried. So let's focus on you."

"Let's not," Emily declared. She set the bag of beans on the floor. "Much as I want to go to prom, I really do *not* want to be a pity case. I'll either go on my terms or I won't go at all. I am *not* going to get desperate."

Charlie's eyes widened. "Sheesh. Touché." He poured himself a mug of coffee, then immediately poured it down the drain. "God, I'm bored," he declared again. He repeated his pour-coffee-dump-coffee routine. "Let's talk about what you'll wear to prom when you find your date."

"Here's a thought." Emily grabbed the mug out of Charlie's hands and set it in the dishwater. She loved working with Charlie—he was a thousand times more normal than Edna, the close-talking day-shift manager—but she had come to realize he was virtually useless and actually created work instead of doing work.

Luckily they almost always shared the evening shift, when demand for tea and coffee was low. They were never very busy, and usually work was just a good excuse to stand around and gossip. "Maybe you could go in back and check inventory on leaves. We should probably fill the canisters out here and put in an order for the stuff we're low on." She wanted to change the subject away from prom, and knew Charlie would just keep bringing it up if she didn't get rid of him.

Charlie lifted his arms over his head and cheered. "I'm on it! I'll be in back if you need me." As he pushed through the swinging door, Emily watched him pull his iPod out of his pocket and spin through his playlists. She doubted he would even bother checking inventory—Charlie had come to realize that whatever he didn't do during the evening shift, the morning shift would take care of the next day.

Emily bent down to pour tea leaves into one of the huge glass canisters on the shelf beneath the front counter. When she stood up again, her breath caught in her throat as a living incarnation of Prince Charming strolled past the Leaf Lounge's open storefront. She stared in admiration at his profile and held her breath when he stopped just outside the entrance to the lounge.

Let it be said that Emily usually didn't go for the quarterback look. But as Prince Charming walked through the doors and leaned against the counter, Emily gained a newfound appreciation for sandy blond hair, chiseled cheekbones, and long, lean muscles tucked under a black T-shirt. His body screamed strong, but his face murmured soft, sensitive, and oh-so-perfect.

It had only been five seconds, and Emily was already in love.

"How's the chai?" he asked, staring above Emily's head at the menu posted on the wall.

Emily twirled her long, shiny black hair around her finger, putting on her biggest flirt. Her hair was her greatest weapon, and she had every intention of using it. "Give it a try," she responded with a coy smile, realizing too late that she was being neither clever nor charming.

But the hottie smiled back, flashing his teeth at her! (Okay, maybe it was just a really big smile that got all shiny in the neon lights of the menu—because, really, whose teeth actually flash?) "I'll take one."

Emily pulled a glass off the shelf. "For here, right?"

"To go," he answered, but Emily thought she saw him pause. "I have to get home. I'm supposed to compose a sonnet for AP English by tomorrow. Haven't started." He flushed.

Aha, she mused. *A smartie!* She replaced the glass and pulled a paper cup off the stack next to the register. "Oh. Well, good luck with that." Emily foamed the milk for his chai while digging for another line of conversation. She finally settled on, "Do you go to Humphrey? You don't look familiar." She knew he didn't go to her high school—and knew she hadn't been required to write a sonnet for her own AP English class—but asking about school was always safe.

"No, I don't go to Humphrey. I was checking out the tux shop—you know, prom."

"Oh," Emily looked down. *Of course he has a girlfriend,* she thought. *Why wouldn't he be going to prom?* "Right."

He rested his elbows on the countertop, leaning over the counter toward Emily. "I'm going with one of my sister's friends, which sounds pretty sad, I guess." Emily didn't think that sounded sad at all—it sounded like hope. "I was looking forward to it, since I've known her forever and it should be fun going with a friend, but she's sort of making me regret asking her." Emily frowned—she was torn between feeling ecstatic that he wasn't going to prom with the love of his life, and sort of disgusted that he was dissing on his date.

The guy continued, laughing. The corners of his eyes got all crinkly, which Emily loved. "That came out wrong. The thing is, I didn't realize she would have all these rules about what I can wear. She wants me to rent this tux she saw in a magazine that has some sort of lining that matches her dress color exactly. I guess I'm a little irritated, since this is the fifth tux shop I've been to that doesn't carry the style. I'm starting to run out of time."

"You know where you could check?" Emily said, stirring chai tea into the foam cup of hot, frothy milk. "There's this vintage shop downtown that has the weirdest mix of stuff. Formal wear, vintage hats, Victorian gowns—they have a sign on the door that says 'We've got what you're looking for and more,' or something like that. I bet they could order it, even if they don't have it in stock. They're pretty helpful. It's worth a look, right?"

"Thanks for the tip." He smiled. Emily thought she caught him checking her out. *Woo hoo,* she thought happily. She twisted her hair and flipped it over one shoulder.

"I'll check it out," he said, nodding appreciatively. She wished he was talking about her, but knew he was referring to the store.

Emily set the cup of chai on the counter. "Whipped cream?"

"Please."

"I'm Emily, by the way."

"I know." Emily furrowed her brow. "Your name tag," he explained.

Emily squirted whipped cream on the

drink—it sprayed out too quickly, and a big glob plopped off the hot drink and landed in a messy splat on the counter. She reddened. Prince Charming didn't seem to notice. He was staring at Emily in a very, very positive way. *Maybe I have hope of finding a prom date after all,* she mused. *We would look fine together.*

"I'm Ethan. Thanks for your help, Emily."

"No prob." She wiped a blob of whipped cream off the outside of the cup and handed it to Ethan. He was watching her face carefully as he grabbed the cup.

"I've never done this before, but . . ." Ethan looked down and took a quick sip of his chai. Emily waited for him to continue. "Do you think you'd want to go out sometime?"

Emily grinned, trying to reign in her excitement. Better not to seem too desperate. "Definitely. I'd love that. Why don't you give me your number?" Emily hadn't ever asked a guy for his number before, but decided it was a cool way to play it. It made her seem much less eager, and put her in charge of how this would go down.

"Oh—okay." Ethan seemed a little

taken off guard. But he scribbled his number on a paper napkin and shoved it across the counter. "Promise you'll call?"

"I promise." Emily grinned and put on a flirty smile. "I guess if I don't, you'll get the hint." She laughed. Visions of her and Ethan walking arm in arm into her prom danced wildly through her head. She knew she was getting ahead of herself, but just couldn't help it.

Ethan smiled back. "I guess I will. Well, see you, Emily." Then he turned and retreated into the fluorescent lights of the mall. Emily was staring off after him, transfixed, when Charlie emerged from the back room.

He let out a long, low whistle, squinting to see Emily's Prince Charming as he pushed through the mall exit. "Nice one. Your team or mine?"

"Definitely mine." Emily broke her stare. She turned toward Charlie just as he grabbed a napkin (*the* napkin) off the counter and hastily wiped up the melting pile of whipped cream that had toppled off Ethan's chai latte a few minutes before. She grabbed his arm to stop him, but it was too late.

When Emily opened the napkin, searching desperately for ten clear digits, the phone number Ethan had just given her had melted into a big, creamy blue blob. Ethan would be getting the hint—just not the one Emily had intended.

Two

Like a good suburban teen, Emily spent Saturday mornings mowing the precisely rectangular lawn of her parents' split-level house. She got paid five dollars, but she probably would have done it for free. She liked the alone time.

It was the first truly warm spring day, and Emily was enjoying herself. She loved to crank up her iPod and sing along to Jack Johnson or Mason Jennings (her favorite local Minnesota artist) as she marched back and forth across the patch of grass. She could shut out the sounds of her boring suburban neighborhood and pretend she was somewhere—anywhere—else.

She had never quite belonged in Minnesota. It's not that there was anything wrong with her home state, exactly—she had just always known, deep down, that she would flee to a land far, far away as soon as she had the opportunity. She couldn't wait to escape.

Emily had set her sights on NYU in middle school after getting hooked on reruns of *Felicity*, and had studied like crazy to get her SAT scores high enough to ensure that she would get in and get a scholarship. Sure enough, she had gotten a thick, manila package several months ago, welcoming her as a partially-subsidized member of NYU's class of 2011. She had another three months of living in her parents' suburban prison before she fled the confines of the Midwest for the fabulousness of New York.

She was counting the hours (2,168 when she last checked) until she and her dad would set off in their Grand Caravan down I-94 en route to New York. Until then, she was bored bored bored. She and every other senior she knew had a major case of senior slide, and Emily had spent the past two months trying desperately to entertain herself into survival.

"Gooood morning, *mi amore!*" Charlie sauntered up Emily's driveway, sliding his aviator sunglasses into place over his eyes. Emily waved, flipping the switch on the mower to off and bluntly kicking the back to release the chunks of grass that were stuck behind the front left wheel.

"Can't I get one morning away from you?" Emily and Charlie had finished their shift at the Leaf Lounge less than twelve hours before and were both scheduled to be back at work that afternoon.

"You know you missed me, love." Charlie grinned and gave his cousin a squeeze. "What'd you make me for breakfast?"

"Make your own damn breakfast, you lazy piece of sh—shingle." Sidney, Charlie's best friend, jumped out the passenger side of Charlie's blue 1986 Volvo. "Hey, Em. Hope you don't mind me crashing here this afternoon." Sid slammed the car door closed, cursing loudly when the window slid open. She glared at Charlie. "Your parents are loaded, you lazy moron. Get a new freakin' car."

Charlie's car functioned, but just barely. When a door was closed on the Volvo, another one opened. And not in the metaphorical sense. Literally, closing one door on the car caused a chain reaction of another door popping open, or a window sliding down. The car was falling apart, but Charlie loved it, in part because it always got Sid so worked up. She had a raging temper and no patience, which kept Charlie amused.

"Rich parents do not a rich kid make." Charlie winked over the top rim of his glasses. "She's so crabby these days," he stage-whispered to Emily. "I don't even know why I bring her out in public. It's embarrassing."

Sid grimaced and pulled her guitar out of the Volvo's trunk. "You know what's embarrassing?" She settled in on Emily's lawn to tune her guitar. Sid was an amazing songwriter and singer and brought her guitar everywhere. Charlie said it was like they had a live soundtrack to accompany them wherever they went—he liked to call it *Charlie: The Musical*. After a beat, Sid continued. "Those aviators are one hundred percent 2005. I don't read *Vogue*, and even I know that," she snapped. "Catch up on your fashion, Charlie. *That's* embarrassing."

Charlie and Sidney were an interesting

pair, to say the least. They always came as a team, and they always bickered. They were like an old married couple: They clearly loved each other, but constantly teased each other.

Unlike Emily, who was a senior at Humphrey High School in the middle of a converted cow field, Sid and Charlie both went to South High. South was a public school that looked like an Ivy League college smushed together with Julliard. Thanks to favorable zoning laws, South drew all the rich, downtown kids with arty, liberal parents and four years of college tuition socked away in savings bonds.

Charlie was the perfect poster child for South. Always groomed, always the lead in the school plays (though never the musicals—Charlie's singing would easily have made the telecast for the worst *American Idol* auditions), always quick with a witty one-liner and clever comment. And his parents—Emily's aunt and uncle—were rich beyond belief. But they had worked for their money, and believed that Charlie needed to learn to manage money himself.

Thus, he was forced to take a job at the Leaf Lounge.

Charlie hated working. But he hated going without even more. Charlie spent every penny he had on clothes, dinners out, and iTunes downloads, knowing his parents would have his back when he got to college.

Emily's parents had gone the opposite route. Her mom, Elizabeth—Charlie's mom's sister—became a high school English teacher after college and married the history teacher in the classroom next to hers.

And so it was that Emily was born into a modest life of literature and long walks rather than wine tastings (Charlie) or summers in Italian villas (also Charlie). Not to mention parents who thought it would be the epitome of cool to give their child a name one syllable away from the writer Emily Brontë.

Emily pulled the mower into the back corner of the garage and pushed her damp bangs off her forehead. Charlie and Sid were still bickering, but both had settled comfortably into plastic lounge chairs they positioned around Emily's little sister's Dora the Explorer plastic pool in the backyard.

"Lemonade would make my life *perfect*, Em." Charlie touched his fingers to his lips and made a kissing motion. "*Che delicioso!* My spa away from home."

"You know your way around—*mi casa es su casa.*" Emily pulled her long black hair into a low knot at the nape of her neck and shoved a stick into the chunk of hair to keep it in place. "You're the one who decided to come way out to no-man's-land today. You know I hate hanging out at my place. So if we add things up, you owe me for letting you come over in the first place. I'll take my lemonade with ice, thanks."

Most weekends, Emily got a lift into the city to chill at Charlie's family's loft downtown. Then in the evenings, they'd relax at Jitters, a cozy downtown coffee shop, to listen to live music, or go to the local bowling alley, Urban Bowl. Nights usually ended at Burrito Jack's for chili con queso and chips.

But lately Charlie had decided that Emily's family's suburban life was quaint, and declared that it was a hoot to hang out at her house—even though his family's loft had direct skywalk access to a bar with darts and foosball. Really, there was no comparison.

Emily could think of nothing more boring than spending one extra minute at her house, but Charlie was the one with his own car . . . so he usually decided where they would hang out. Charlie almost always got his way. It's just the way their relationship worked. And he was currently on a "bland suburbs=rockin' good time" kick.

"While you're inside, grab me a Pop-Tart, will you?" Sid batted her long eyelashes at Charlie, who looked like he had no intention of going anywhere. She hummed and plucked a string on her guitar, singing, "Pop-Tarts, Pop-Tarts. Strawberry Pop-Tarts."

"You're already up, Em," Charlie whined. "Why don't you just run along and grab us some snacks and drinks?" Emily's cousin was persistent, and equally lazy. Though Emily had no interest in waiting on him, she knew Charlie wouldn't stop begging for the next hour.

Just as she was about to head inside to grab a pitcher of lemonade to shut him up, she spotted Max, her neighbor and best friend since forever, trekking across the cul-de-sac. She lifted her arm to wave.

"Perfect timing, my friend," Charlie shouted in Max's direction. "I was just about to run inside to get us some lemonade—

could you be a love and detour past the kitchen to grab something tasty to drink? Since you're already up, obviously. An object in motion likes to stay in motion, right?" He glanced around, seeking approval. "Inertia."

Emily rolled her eyes in Max's direction. He laughed, familiar with Charlie's requests. The four of them had been hanging out a lot in the past few months. Charlie and Sid had always been friends, as had Max and Emily. But it was only after going out as a group the previous New Year's Eve that they all started hanging out regularly as a foursome. They complemented one another well.

"You got it," Max responded. "Can I bring you a cooling eye mask or a personal masseuse to go with that, King Charlie?"

"Strawberry Pop-Tart, please!" Sid called as Max pushed open Emily's front door. "Thank you, Max. You're a *lurve*."

Max and Emily had been friends since the day a five-year-old Emily had run around the neighborhood wearing only Scooby Doo underwear and baby powder, shouting, "I'm Snow White! I'm Snow White!" Her family had just moved to the block, and Emily's parents were less than impressed with her self-introduction to the neighborhood. People had learned a little more about Emily that day than anyone cared to remember.

After baby Emily's afternoon adventure, her parents had felt it necessary to make a more modest introduction to each of their neighbors later that evening. So they had strolled around the hood, Emily dressed in a green gingham dress, and shaken hands with all the parents. Emily coyly stuck her tongue out at each kid who hid behind his or her parents' knees.

Most of the neighborhood kids had been well trained and knew they ought not reciprocate the gesture. Only Max had been bold enough to stick his tongue out in return and blow a raspberry in her direction. It was this little joint rebellion that bonded them as instant friends.

"Voilà!" Max had returned from the kitchen with a Pop-Tart and a glass of lemonade on a plate that he had covered with an upside down mixing bowl. He presented the plate to Charlie, fancy restaurant-style. "Bon appétit!"

"That's what I call service," Charlie

remarked, pulling the bowl off his plate and nodding his approval. "I like."

Max snorted. "And for the ladies—" He presented two plastic SpongeBob cups filled with lemonade that he held clumsily with two fingers of his other hand, and produced a second package of Pop-Tarts from his back pocket.

"What about you?" Emily asked as Max sat down on the ground with his feet resting in the inflatable pool. "You just schlepped all this stuff out here for my charming cousin and didn't get yourself anything?"

"Not thirsty," Max said simply, closing his eyes and tilting his face up toward the sun. "I'm trying the grapefruit diet for a day, so I'm already nice and hydrated." Emily laughed and rolled her eyes. Max was always doing weird things like "trying the grapefruit diet for a day" or entering the John Beargrease Sled Dog Marathon.

On the outside, Max was a completely normal suburban guy—a cute, medium-tall teen with slightly too-long brown hair and Abercrombie style. But his friends knew he was an aspiring journalist, and that he always chased potential—and often bizarre—story ideas wholeheartedly. Emily could only imagine the grapefruit diet had something to do with a story pitch he was working on.

Charlie studied his Pop-Tart package and held it out at arm's length toward Sidney. "Sid—trade?"

She studied him suspiciously. "Why?"

"Mine's crushed."

"Please tell me you're kidding." Sid stared at Charlie in disbelief. "Who the he—heck crowned you prom king?"

One could always count on Sid to say it like it is. Charlie liked to push people's buttons, but Sid always let him know when he'd taken it one step too far.

"Speaking of prom," Charlie said, artfully changing the subject, "Marisa Sanchez is freaking."

"Who's Marisa Sanchez?" Max asked, only half interested. "And we care about prom why?"

Charlie gasped dramatically. "Marisa Sanchez is only *the* most sure-to-win prom queen candidate in the history of South High. But I heard a rumor"—he paused for effect—"that she was busted with a bottle of Jack at Lainie Callen's Roller Derby party last week and got kicked off the prom committee."

Sid giggled. Sid *never* giggled. Though she was short and petite and perky-looking (you could almost go so far as to say she resembled a cheerleader—gasp), Sid was much more pit bull than poodle. Giggling just did not fit her image. "This is especially funny since Marisa Sanchez is the girl that busted me for smoking a Marlboro outside the gym doors instead of rah-rahing at last fall's homecoming pep rally." Sid sighed contentedly and strummed a melancholy chord on her guitar. "Karma, bi—bella, karma."

"Sidney, Sidney . . ." Charlie jokingly tsk-tsked at Sid and took a long sip of lemonade. "Your vow to stop swearing is *not* going so well." Sid was as skilled at swearing as she was at singing, but had decided two months earlier to abandon her potty mouth. Charlie thought it was hilarious, particularly when Sid *started* to swear, then switched her words at the last minute.

Sid rolled her eyes. "Did I swear?" She narrowed her eyes at Charlie. "No, I did not. In fact I called Marisa Sanchez, prom queen extraordinaire, *bella* . . . beautiful. I am a sweetheart."

"Speaking of prom—again," Emily said,

attempting to head off another bickering session between Charlie and Sid, "I have a date."

Her three friends turned. The looks on their faces suggested disbelief.

"What?" she said, smiling mischievously. "You don't believe me?"

"We're with you constantly," Charlie said in response. "When would you have had time to get yourself a date that we wouldn't know about?"

"Let me clarify. I have a date, if I can *find* him again."

"You do or you don't have a date?" Max looked confused and a little ill. The grapefruit seemed to be messing with him.

"I met the guy last night at the mall. His name is Ethan."

"Cut!" Charlie yelled, clinking the ice cubes in his empty lemonade glass over his head like a maraca. "I was *there*, remember? You don't even have his number, if I'm not mistaken. My apologies for that."

Charlie had already apologized a million times for his goof the night before. After Emily had run out the mall doors after Ethan and searched the parking lot until she was sure he was nowhere to be found, she and Charlie couldn't help but laugh a little.

Emily lifted her hand. "Clarification. I *had* his number. But you're correct—I no longer have his number. Which means we have some plotting to do."

"Is this another Emily plan?" Max asked, leaning his head back into the grass. He waved his fingers in the air and chanted, "Go, Tigers! Yay!" He was referring to Emily's sophomore-year plot to try out for the cheerleading squad, even though she hated cheerleading. She just thought it would be funny. "Because honestly, your plans sort of scare me." Like he was one to talk.

"Ding, ding, ding!" Emily replied, clapping. "I have a plan."

She continued, "Here's what I know about this guy. One: He is going to prom because he was shopping for his tux. And PS, he's going with his sister's friend, not a girlfriend, and he was definitely flirting with me—so this isn't some delusional one-way street. Two: His name is Ethan. Three: He doesn't go to Humphrey." She paused, flicking a leaf that had floated over her foot in the wading pool. "So . . . we go where we know he will be! Let's find a way to get into all the other proms in the city and find this guy."

"Oh my God. It reminds me of *Wedding Crashers*," Charlie said, grinning. He had a major celebrity crush on Owen Wilson. Which wasn't surprising, considering the fact that Charlie was completely narcissistic and actually looked a little bit like Owen Wilson. It was like he had a crush on himself. "We are going to be *Prom* Crashers!" He looked thrilled.

"So does this mean you're in?" Emily asked hopefully.

Charlie nodded. "Absolutely."

Emily looked at the other two expectantly.

"What?" Sid asked. "You have Charlie. Why do you need me?"

Max grunted from his post on the ground. "What she said."

"You guys!" Emily stuck out her foot and rolled Max onto his side on the grass so he was facing her. "We have to do this together. One last fling before we all take off for college. The ultimate challenge. What do you say?"

"I say"—Sid chewed her Pop-Tart with her mouth open—"screw prom. I'm not going to my own—why would I want to go to someone else's?"

Charlie pushed his lip out in a pout. "I need you, Sid."

"Forget it," Emily retorted. "I'm not begging. But it's going to be a blast. That's all I'm saying. I know that *I* need something to get me through the rest of this year. I mean, this is the last month or whatever of our last year of high school. It would have been fun to go out in style, the four of us, you know?" She blew her bangs out of her face and crossed her arms over her chest. "Whatever. You guys can spend the next month studying by yourselves. Charlie and I are going to rock crashing proms. Harumph." She had a faint smile tugging at the corners of her mouth.

Sid shrugged and glanced at Max. "Fine. I'm in." She grinned meekly. "When you put it that way."

"Nuh-uh." Emily shook her finger. "Not like that. If you're in, you're in. No half-hearted 'fine.'" She made quotes in the air.

Charlie snickered. "Tough guy. I like it."

"I'm in! I'm in!" Sid sarcastically cheered her arms in the air. "Better? I'll take anything to kill the time until we graduate.

It sounds sort of fun." She shrugged. "Besides, you literally couldn't drag me to my own prom. So this is a good way to see what this prom crap is all about. Do I get to wear pink?"

"I'll do it on one condition," Max broke in, pushing himself up on his elbows on the ground. He was laughing at the image of Sid in pink.

"Yes?" Emily prompted. She was giddy with the hope that this might actually happen. She could think of no better way to celebrate prom season—and get a date— than with a crazy challenge.

Max looked at Emily sternly. "This is about the quest. I couldn't care less about finding this guy—it just sounds like a good time. You promise you won't get all serious and psychostalker?"

"Come on. . . . Who would be more into the adventure than me? This is totally about the quest." She looked innocent and laughed when Max continued to look at her sharply.

"Fine," he agreed. "But promise anyway. This is *not* just about the guy."

She nodded seriously. "I promise. Of

course I *want* to find Ethan. But prom crashing is the perfect distraction to kill the time before we get out of this lame town. And if we succeed in our mission, I will have a superfoxy date. What could be better than that?"

Three

"We have nine targets." Charlie had spread paper beverage napkins across the counter at the Leaf Lounge. Each napkin had the name of one of the local high schools written on it. He and Emily were working the Wednesday night shift, and Charlie had spent most of it plotting their first move for Operation Prom Crashing.

Max, who was sitting on Frank's stool at the counter, had come to the mall partly to plan, partly to flesh out his latest story pitch (a feature about some local guy who carved bears out of cheese rind), and partly to catch the tail end of Sid's set.

Sid often played her guitar and sang in the evenings at the Leaf Lounge. Gary thought she gave the place a cool vibe, and Sid was happy to have the venue. She was trying to get her start somewhere, and while she realized the mall coffee shop wasn't the Knitting Factory in New York, at least it gave her practice playing in front of a live crowd.

As was often the case, though, the "crowd" was only two people strong—Max, of course, and Vern, a cashier from Dylan's, the mall department store, who had hustled over to hear her play during his break. Vern always came to Sid's sets—he fashioned himself her biggest fan. He was maybe her *only* nonfriend fan. Sid's ultimate goal was to spend her life touring the country to play small clubs in big cities. But the first step was to extend her reach beyond the mall's four walls and gain a slightly cooler fan base.

Her bluesy-rock sound was fabulous. She just needed her break.

As Sid struck the final chord for her last song, Vern broke into mad applause. Emily rolled her eyes. Sid dropped her guitar into its case and strolled over to the counter, with a brief nod in Vern's direction.

"Complimentary beverage?" Emily asked. "Great set."

"Coffee?" Sid grabbed one of the napkins off the counter and studied it. She didn't like to talk about her performances—she always said that the lack of audience was painfully depressing. "What's all this?"

"All this," Charlie explained, "is the beginning of a plan. Did everyone do their research this week?"

The other three nodded. After agreeing to Emily's prom crashing plan the previous weekend, each of them had contacted everyone they knew, trying to get intelligence about all the other proms around the city so that they could formulate a plan. As they reported their findings, Charlie pulled out each school's napkin and scribbled out the date and location of its prom.

Emily studied the napkins and began to sort them into piles. "We have four weekends. Nine proms."

"We can count out our own schools," Max said, plucking the napkins with South and Humphrey written on them. "We know Ethan won't be there, right? Charlie, Sid, you checked South's directory for an Ethan?" Charlie nodded. "So that's only seven. Not bad."

Sid slapped her hand on the counter. "Totally doable."

"We have a big weekend ahead of us," Emily said, grinning. "Three this Saturday—Marshall, Park, and Memorial."

"Like, three days from now?" Max asked, sounding mildly concerned.

"Yup. You worried?" Emily poked him in the arm. He poked her back. Emily hoped he was eating real food again and not just grapefruit, otherwise he'd be really crabby for their first proms.

Charlie shuffled three of the napkins so that they were lined up in front of him on the counter. "All right," he said, suddenly very businesslike. "What's our strategy for these first three? Do we just break in? Show up? How are we gonna do this?"

Emily chewed her lower lip thoughtfully. "Well, I guess we could just sneak in," she said finally. "Though that seems a little boring."

"And not possible at Memorial," Sid said, sipping her coffee. "The guy I know who goes there said security is really tight on the day of prom. The dance itself is held in Memorial's gym. They lock all the doors a few hours before prom starts to keep the unsavory types out. And it's a superstrict ticket system. I guess the parents all get paranoid for their precious babies' security."

"Okay." Emily nodded. "So sneaking in isn't an option at Memorial. Maybe we could plant someone on the inside before they lock the doors?"

Charlie clapped. "I like that!"

"The other two are both at the convention center," Max broke in. He had found the details about Marshall and Park's proms online. "So maybe we divide and conquer? Two of us go to Marshall and Park, the other two to Memorial?"

"Yeah," Emily said, "that would be good, except I'm the only one who knows what Ethan looks like. The point of our mission, remember?"

Max rolled his eyes. "Ah, yes . . . the guy."

"Ethan," Emily corrected. "Plus, isn't this more fun if we all do it together? Max, what if you and I try to break into Marshall and Park, then meet up with Sid and Charlie at Memorial later? They could sneak into the school that afternoon and hang out, then let us in through an unguarded door when we get there?"

"Nice." Charlie waved the napkin with Memorial written on it. "My first conquest."

Sid raised her hand. "One other tiny issue," she said, waiting to get their attention. "I have nothing to wear."

"I can borrow my dad's tux," Max declared proudly. "It might be a little big and boxy, but it's free. If I'm not going to my own prom, I'm not paying to rent one." Max didn't have a date for prom. He and Emily had sort of joked about going together, but neither had actually bought tickets.

"I own a tux, so I'm good," Charlie said. "I feel tacky wearing the same shirt more than once, but I guess since it will be different crowds at each prom, I can break the rule."

Emily and Sid exchanged a look. "Since I'm not *officially* going to prom—yet—it might be a little tough to convince my parents to buy me a dress. I'd have to do too much explaining. How about you, Sid?"

"Nothing. And I'm not borrowing from my mom. Nuh-uh. No freakin' way. She wears shoulder pads."

"So we can either buy something or go with what we have. We'll obviously look out of place in jeans, which makes crashing a little more challenging. Don't we need to fit in to get in?"

Sid nodded. "I'm going to propose a third option, since I refuse to buy a prom dress." She jumped off her stool. "Max, can you cover for Em? Charlie doesn't do anything, and someone has to serve the customers while I steal Emily for two secs."

"Hey!" Charlie feigned anger, but knew he had no right to be defensive.

"I don't even know what a green tea latte is," Max responded. "But yeah, I can cover." He moved behind the counter as Emily slid past him and untied her apron.

"What's the plan?" she asked as Sid pulled her into the mall.

"You're about to see me do something *very* scary. If you laugh, I'll bite. I mean it." Emily promised to keep a straight face, and she followed Sid into the mall's department store.

Sid sauntered up to Vern, whose break had ended and who now stood sorting hangers behind the counter in the young men's department. "Hey, Vern." Vern looked up, a huge smile spreading across his face as Sid leaned in toward him. "Thanks for coming to hear me play tonight."

"Oh, uh, no problem," Vern said, obviously taken aback by Sid approaching him.

"What'd you think of the set?"

"Good," Vern replied, lowering his voice. It cracked slightly under the pressure. "You were great."

"Thanks, babe." Sid smiled suggestively. "I love that you always come to my shows. It means a lot to me."

Vern flushed and nodded. "Yeah, well, your singing means a lot to me. You look so confident up there."

Emily's head flipped back and forth like she was watching a tennis match as Sid expertly charmed and wooed Vern. She was highly impressed with—and surprised by—Sid's flirting skills.

"So," Sid said, elbows resting on the counter in front of Vern. "I have a teeny-tiny favor to ask. Do you think you could help me out? It would mean the *world* to me."

Vern stuttered. "Oh, ah, sure. What's up?"

Sid was twisting her shortish, caramel-colored hair between two fingers. A dyed-red streaky piece fell across her left eye.

Vern stared at it, entranced. "The thing is, Emily and I are both going to prom. Together, as friends, of course—I don't believe in prom dates. It's so stifling." She glanced at Emily. "Anyway, neither of us has anything to wear. And I'm saving up for a new guitar." Sid broke off momentarily. "You will come hear me play it, right?"

Vern nodded, mouth slightly agape.

"Do you think there's any chance you might let us *borrow* dresses from Dylan's? We would clean them and return them as soon as we're done." Sid leaned in closer for her last line. "No one would need to know."

Emily stared, transfixed. She could only imagine how Vern was feeling at that moment.

"Um." Vern looked around to make sure no other clerks were within earshot. "It would be our little secret?"

"Our little secret," Sid confirmed, nodding.

"I guess it couldn't hurt anyone, right?" Vern's face cracked a smile. "Follow me."

Sid grabbed Emily's hand and gave it a squeeze as the two of them followed Vern through a set of double doors marked EMPLOYEES ONLY. When they reached the back room, Vern turned to face them with a huge grin. "Take your pick. I'll guard the doors. Do you think you can find something?"

Emily and Sid stared around at the racks and shelves of dresses hanging, folded, and boxed up, ready to be moved out to the floor. They both nodded, and Vern retreated, leaving them alone with their personal dress collection.

"I feel so sleazy," Sid groaned.

"Sidney Cristina Martinez, you are a flirt. A good one."

"If you blab, just kill me first. I'm not proud."

Emily laughed. "I promise not to tell." She flipped through a rack of dresses, searching for the size tens. There were only tiny sizes on the rack. Emily had always wondered who fit into the size zeros and twos— she was tall and lanky, with broad shoulders she had developed during her years as a competitive swimmer, and couldn't remember *ever* being a zero.

"Do you see any twos?" Sid asked, flipping through a rack across the room.

Emily groaned inwardly. "Yeah, over here." *So size twos do exist,* she thought. Sid was short and compact and absolutely adorable—until she opened her mouth. Then she was a size twenty-four.

Sid pulled off her T-shirt, revealing her black sports bra, and slid a Pepto-Bismol-pink A-line dress over her head. She gagged loudly before pulling the dress back over her head. "Prom sucks." She stood half-naked, selecting another dress to try on.

"Why are you so antiprom?" Emily asked, considering a magenta dress hanging on the rack in front of her.

"Why are you so not?" Sid retorted with a smile. "Seriously, what is it about prom that makes you so blubbery?"

Emily raised an eyebrow. "Blubbery? That's a flattering choice of words." Sid shrugged. "I don't know. . . . I guess I've always had this romantic image of prom night, with flowers and pictures and kissing and dancing. There's just something sweet about it all."

"Oh, come on," Sid blurted out. "It's a totally old-fashioned custom that needs to die."

"You sound like Marco." Emily thought back to her conversation with Charlie a few days earlier. She knew her cousin believed in prom almost as much as she did—so it was unfortunate that both his boyfriend and his best friend were so antiestablishment on the prom front. "You have to admit that getting dressed up and swooped off into a limo with a total hottie sounds fun."

"Sure." Sid poked her head through the loose neck of a strapless orange gown. "If you're getting picked up by your hot best friends and going to prom for a laugh. You can get me on board for that—but prom for real? Nope." She laughed at the orange dress—which made her look like a Caribbean cocktail come to life—and quickly unzipped it. "Speaking of friends and prom . . . I've always sort of wanted to ask you this." She threw the orange gown back on a hanger. "Why haven't you and Max ever . . . you know . . ." She winked. "Isn't this your big chance with him? You have seven proms to make it official."

Emily grimaced. People always asked if she and Max were hooking up. They had been friends forever, but it had never felt right. "I don't know. I guess we're just better friends. There's never been an attraction like that."

"Have either of you ever even *dated*

anyone else? Maybe there's secret lust just sitting there, undiscovered."

Emily shook her head. "No secret lust. And yeah, I've dated people. Just no one decent. Slobbery-tongue Dan was my low period."

"What about Max? Does he have a hot history?" Sid pulled a sleeveless amethyst gown over her head.

"No, Max has been single forever. But that doesn't mean anything."

"Uh-huh. What do you think?" Sid asked, referring to the dress. The deep blue and sleek fabric complimented her medium-brown skin perfectly, and the cut made her look like a superstar.

Emily gave her a thumbs-up. "Perfect. You look like a tiny little model."

"Hey, bi—butterscotch! Tiny, I'll take. Little, no way. I'm tough. You having any luck over there?" Sid strolled over toward Emily's racks, her slouchy jeans sticking out the bottom of her dress. She pulled an emerald green cocktail dress off the rack and stood on her toes to slide it, still on its hanger, over Emily's head.

"So?" Emily prompted.

"Cute. But you can do better." Sid

selected a rich pink shimmery satin gown from a box on the floor. "Take off your shirt," she instructed.

Emily slid her coffee-stained shirt over her head and pulled the dress on in its place. The material draped seductively over her chest and clung to her slim hips, making her look half her original size. Sid whistled.

"You look like a pink Oscar statue. Hot." She studied Emily's figure wrapped into the pink material and growled. "Really hot."

"So this is the one?" Suddenly prom felt more real to Emily than ever before. She could see Ethan's smile, could feel his arms wrapped around her on the dance floor. She imagined their good-night kiss.

"That's it. When we find Ethan, he's going to be drooling."

Emily grinned and squeezed Sid into a hug. "That's the point, isn't it?"

Sid and Emily strolled happily back to the Leaf Lounge, dresses tucked under their arms in Dylan's bags. As they approached the shop's entrance, Neil, the clerk at the jewelry kiosk in the middle of the mall's corridor, called out to Emily. Sid hustled past, back into the Leaf Lounge, leaving Emily to fend for herself.

"Hey, Neil." Neil had asked Emily out once a week since she had started at the Leaf Lounge the year before. His parents owned the kiosk, so he worked most nights. He had greasy flaked hair, a rude attitude, and undeterred confidence. Neil was not her type. At all. Ever. "How's it going?"

"Good, good." Neil ran his fingers through his hair, releasing a storm cloud of flakes. "What'cha got there?" He pointed to her bag.

"Oh. Prom dress."

Neil stared. "Who's the lucky guy?"

"It's a long story, actually." Emily suddenly realized something. "What school do you go to again?" She already knew the answer.

"Marshall." He narrowed his eyes. "Why?"

"No reason. Isn't your prom this weekend? Who are you taking?" Emily mentally crossed her fingers. This was a long shot, but she was suddenly realizing she may have an in at her very first prom.

Neil blushed. "I . . . ah . . . I'm not going." He looked sad and a little vulnerable.

"Why not?" Emily feigned surprise. She

moved in closer to Neil, groaning inwardly. *Sacrifices, sacrifices,* she thought.

"Couldn't find the right girl."

"That's crazy!" Emily blurted out, feeling only slightly guilty. *I am a terrible person.* "Do you *want* to go?"

Neil's face brightened. He was beginning to catch on. "Hey! You should go with me."

"I don't even go to your school," Emily said, not caring in the least.

"That's perfect!" Neil exclaimed. Emily realized she would be arm candy—no one would know who she was, and it would make Neil look like he was some sort of stud outside school walls, since she could only imagine he wasn't the coolest guy at Marshall. *But you never know,* she mused. Neil looked giddy. "I mean, it doesn't matter if you don't go to Marshall. It would be fun. Whaddaya say?"

"Yeah, okay. Can I get your number?" This would be a perfect arrangement—she could give Neil girl credibility with his friends; he would be her in at prom number one.

Neil grinned in a way that made Emily feel a little oozy. "Sure, babe."

"Neil." Emily leaned over the counter. "Do not call me babe. We're not there yet."

He flushed. "Got it." Neil scribbled his number on a piece of Dress Yourself in Diamante stationery. "Should I pick you up at seven?"

"Oh." She didn't want Neil to know where she lived, nor did she want her parents to find out about this. The image of Neil pulling up in her driveway and shaking hands with Mr. and Mrs. Bronson while Emily paraded down the stairs in her prom dress made her want to gag. She'd have to get ready at Charlie's and make up some excuse for why she was going out. Prom pictures with Neil were not suitable for the family photo album. "Why don't we just meet here?"

"At the mall?"

"Yeah." Emily nodded. "I'll meet you right here at seven. That's enough time, right?"

"There's never enough time for Neil."

"Right." Emily gritted her teeth, then smiled. "I'll see you Saturday. I'm looking forward to it."

Later that night when Emily got home, she flipped on the computer in her family room. She had a paper due in Honors English the next day and had six scenes left to read in

King Lear before she had any hope of pulling something legible together.

But the last thing she felt like doing was reading the final pages. She would much rather catch up on Gawker Stalker scoop, and her NYU acceptance letter gave her the security of knowing she could coast for the next few weeks.

As she surfed through the day's celebrigossip an IM popped up in the lower-left corner of her computer screen.

M: Hey.

Emily smiled. Max lived next door but always IMed. He was constantly online finding unusual story ideas. In addition to the grapefruit diet and cheese-rind-bear-carving stories, he was also developing a story about yurts—whatever yurts were.

E: hey back.
M: How was the rest of work?
E: so exciting. how's yr story?
M: I'm learning how to make turducken.
E: ??
M: It's a chicken that's cooked in a duck that's cooked in a turkey. Crazy!!

E: i'm a better person for knowing that. tx.

M: What r u up to?

E: wasting time. u?

M: Avoiding my Lear paper.

E: clearly. *sigh*

M: Movie?

E: k. here or there?

M: There in a sec.

Emily smiled and flipped off the computer. She headed toward the kitchen to get a bag of chips. Emily and Max had had at least one movie night a week for as long as she could remember. Max was a freelance movie reviewer for a local online arts website. He was using the movie reviewing to get an in with the editors so that he could work on features and profiles. But he'd been writing reviews for a year and, despite a ton of pitches, had yet to land a feature—though he did get to screen some really bad films. Emily loved to join him and make fun of the worst ones.

She had been thinking a lot lately about what she was going to do next year without their regular movie nights to look forward to. They'd hung out almost every day since third grade. Even when both Emily and Max had been grounded for setting up a bug dissection lab in Max's kitchen—using Max's mom's good silver and china as tools—they had still "chatted" through their secret flashlight communication system. (Both hid flashlights under their mattresses and devised an illogical Morse code to communicate, just in case aliens had taken over their neighborhood.)

Now that college was drawing nearer, Emily wasn't sure what she was going to do when Max was in Appleton, Wisconsin, and she was all the way out in New York. Max poked his head around the corner and peered into the family room. "There you are. Your sister said you weren't home."

"As far as she's concerned, I'm not." Emily's little sister, Abby, was an eight-year-old "accident" who was now just a pain in her butt. Emily often came home from work and quietly tiptoed into the house without greeting anyone. She needed a few minutes of peace before the questions (from her sister) and advice (from her mom) started.

Lately her mom had been on a nonstop prom kick. She hadn't yet accepted the fact that her little girl might not be going. So she left magazines on the coffee table with dog-eared pages showcasing dresses she thought would look good on Emily. Emily didn't know what her mom would do when she found out that she had (a) selected a dress without her mom's guidance (that, PS, she didn't even buy) and (b) decided to go to every prom in the city *except* her own. She hoped to keep her crashing scheme a secret from her family as long as possible.

"I brought *Never Been Kissed*." Max beamed.

Emily smiled. "Perfect." As she nestled into the couch next to her best friend, giggling at the opening scene of the movie, she couldn't keep Sid's question from niggling in the back of her mind. *That's crazy,* she thought, dismissing the idea of her and Max together. This *is perfect*.

Four

The next afternoon, Emily waited for Max at her locker after school. Earlier that day he had stuck a note written on a chewing gum wrapper through her locker door, asking her to wait for him after chemistry class. She had the afternoon off work and knew Max would offer up some distraction to kill the time, so she happily obliged. Max appeared at her locker a few minutes after the last bell with two pairs of roller skates tucked under his arm.

"Uh-oh." Emily nodded toward the roller skates. "What's up?"

Max grinned mischievously. "I need your help."

"I figured as much. What's the plan?"

"New story idea," Max declared. "I'm going to write a piece on the benefits of roller skates. I think they're about to make a comeback. I want to figure out how easy it is to get around on eight wheels."

Emily looked at him, her face blank. "You're serious? What happened to the cheese rind story? And the grapefruit diet stuff? And the turduck—thing?"

"I'm on to new pastures," Max said happily. "Those stories were going nowhere. *This*"—he held a pair of the skates out to Emily—"is going to be a good one."

She grabbed the skates and slammed her locker closed. "You'll drive, right? I was going to take the bus home."

Max nodded. "I'll drive as far as downtown. But then we can only go places we can get to on foot-wheels."

"Okay," Emily agreed. "I'll go on one condition." She twisted her hair into a knot and fastened it with a pencil from her backpack. "As long as we're going downtown . . ."

She paused and Max broke in. "Don't pretend to be difficult. I know you're going to go with me—you always do, and that's why I like you. And you know I'm going to agree to your condition, so what's the use of pretending to play hard to get, Emily B.?"

Emily laughed. "All true." She linked arms with Max as they strode out to the parking lot. "Here's my condition: I want to stop by that little vintage-type shop. You know, the one by the ice cream place? I told Ethan he should check it out, and I want to see if he's been there yet. Maybe we can find out his last name."

"Em, I will agree to your condition"— Max unlocked the car—"provided we can get there on skates."

She grinned. "I feel confident the shop is eight-wheel accessible." They hopped in Max's car, chatting about their day and their upcoming plans for their first prom crash. When they got downtown, Max parked his car at a meter and they fastened their skates. Emily rolled away from the car. "I haven't done this since I was about eight years old."

"Exactly!" Max cried. "But it's a very respectable form of transportation. I think our afternoon will be much more fun on skates."

Emily laughed. Max was a total goofball, and when they were together, he always came up with the weirdest things for them to do. But his ideas only took him so far—Max didn't always have the nerve to go through with his crazy ideas if Emily wasn't around. He needed her nearby to give him the courage to go for it. "Are you ready?" she asked.

They skated down the sidewalk, ignoring the looks they were getting from the businesspeople walking past. Emily stumbled a few times, but Max helped keep her upright. He grabbed her arm as they rolled past a local modern art museum and pulled her into the doorway.

"Should we go in?" he asked, a smile tugging at the corner of his lips. "Quick pit stop?"

"Why not?" Emily shrugged, slightly relieved to get away from the obvious stares of the people on the street. "Will it help your story?" Since she was dragging him to the vintage shop, she figured she owed him a few minutes.

Max nodded seriously. "Most definitely. This is a great example of one of the cool places your wheels can take you. So many people think museums, galleries, what have you, take too long to fully enjoy." He lifted a leg, balancing on one skate. "With roller skates, you can get through the whole museum in, like, ten minutes."

They smiled politely at the guy manning the front desk, who barely even noticed their skates. Student admission was free, so they both flashed their high school IDs and rolled into the first room in the gallery. Emily wheeled sideways behind Max, forming her legs into an awkward plié. She stuck her arms out to her sides to balance and took in all the art passing by in front of her.

After they wheeled through the whole gallery—which had in fact taken less than ten minutes—Max led her back outside. "Where now?"

"Vintage shop," Emily declared. "As agreed."

Max followed as Emily skated down the sidewalk. "What are the odds I'll sell a story someday?" he asked suddenly. "Fifty-fifty? Eighty-twenty?"

"One hundred–zero. Or the other way around—whichever means the odds are for you. You're a great writer. You maybe just need to find your audience. Your stories are a little more niche than editors are accustomed to. For example, how relevant is roller skating in an art gallery?" She wasn't telling Max something he didn't already know. He was aware that his story ideas were out there, but continued to go after the subjects that made him laugh.

"Yeah, okay." Max nodded. "Is this the place?" He gestured to a wooden door set back from the sidewalk.

Emily pulled the door open and started down a narrow set of stairs on her skates. "This is it. Are you coming?" She turned back to Max, who stood at the top of the stairs.

"Yeah," he said slowly, eyeing the steep stairs. "I think I'll just hang out here. Keep an eye on things."

She laughed. "Uh-huh." He really was a chicken. All talk, no do. "I'll be right back." Downstairs, the little shop smelled like a combination of cinnamon and closet. There was a stick of incense burning on the counter, obviously there to mask the smell of old, musty clothes. "Hi," she greeted the clerk, who was a middle-aged guy wearing a fedora.

"What can I do for you?"

Emily rolled gingerly through the packed racks of clothing, approaching the counter. "Strange question," she started.

The guy cut her off. "I doubt it. Try me."

"So I met this guy . . ." She told an abbreviated version of how she'd met Ethan, lost his number, and how she was now trying to find him again. "Anyway, he was looking for a tux for prom, and it was sort of a rare style, so I suggested he check here."

The clerk whistled. "Thanks for the referral. I can give you an extra punch on your loyalty card if you want."

"Oh, you know what, that's okay." Emily looked at him curiously. He thought she had told that story for praise? Yikes. "I was actually wondering if you remember a guy coming in and asking about a tux? I'm sort of hoping you might remember his last name."

"Yeah." The clerk nodded.

"Yeah?" Emily asked hopefully.

"There was some guy in here yesterday afternoon—about this time, maybe. He asked about a tux. Pretty hot, right?" *Ewwww,* Emily thought. The clerk was old enough to be Ethan's dad.

Emily ignored the question. "So he was here? Yesterday?" Her heart sank. Had she come one day earlier, she might have caught him. Talk about meant-to-be.

"Yeah, yesterday. But I didn't get his name. We didn't have the tux, so he left." The clerk extracted a new stick of incense from a small bag under the counter. "Swoosh—off like the wind."

"Oh." Emily's disappointment was obvious. "Well, thanks anyway." She started back to the stairs.

"If it helps," the clerk called after her, "he was wearing a sweatshirt with an *M* on it."

"*M*?" Emily perked up. "Like, *M* for Marshall or Memorial?"—two of the schools' proms they were planning to crash.

"Maybe." He looked strained, as though the process of digging into his memory was a full day's workout. "I do know it said Minnesota on the back."

She sunk again. "So probably more like *M* for Minnesota? Like, University of Minnesota?"

"Yeah, that's what it was."

"Not helpful," Emily muttered, and climbed slowly back up the stairs to meet Max.

"Where have you been, Emily? Why do you have roller skates, Emily?" Emily had walked in to her house less than ten seconds earlier, and her sister had already managed to squeeze in approximately eight hundred questions. "Do I look pretty, Emily?"

Emily ignored all of her sister's questions, choosing instead to ask one of her own. "Where did you get that dress, Abby?" Her little sister was drowning in a sea-foam green lace gown with puffy, pleated sleeves. The dress fell past her ankles and had slid off one of her shoulders. Her hair was combed into two small ponytails over each of her ears. Emily grinned, despite her annoyance at the question barrage. Abby looked really cute.

"Do you like it?" Abby twirled. "Do I look like mom?" She hopped in place, making the dress slip farther off her shoulder. She tripped on the bottom of the dress and fell to the floor in a fit of giggles.

"Oh, Emily, you're home." Emily's mom came into the front hall from the kitchen. She helped Abby up off the floor and slipped the dress back onto her younger daughter's shoulder. "I found my old prom dress! I thought maybe you girls could try it on, just for a laugh. Doesn't Abby look cute?"

Emily groaned. The next four weeks

were going to be really long. "Mom," she warned. "You promised to stop nagging me about prom."

"Oh, honey, don't be so dramatic," her mom chided. "It's just for fun."

"No, Mom, it's not just for fun. You're trying to get me in a prom state of mind so that you can do all your voodoo prom magic on me and try to get me to sit down and look through catalogs with you. I still don't have a date . . . which means I don't want to talk about it and I don't want to shop for a dress."

Abby stared up at Emily, then slipped her mom's dress up and over her head. Under the dress, she was wearing a T-shirt and It's Happy Bunny boxer shorts that said "You'd be cooler if you were me." "Want to try it on, Emily?" she offered. "Don't you think you'd be pretty in Mom's dress? Don't you just love prom?"

"Argh!" Emily kicked off her shoes and walked toward the family room. "I haven't even been home for five minutes, and I'm getting attacked by Mother Prom and her little Promling. Can you guys please, please, just give me a few minutes of peace?" She sighed dramatically. "Besides, that is the ugliest dress on the face of the Earth."

Her mom laughed in the hallway. "We love you, Emily. Don't worry about the dress—sea-foam green really isn't your color anyway. We'll find you the perfect prom dress. Maybe navy?" Emily ignored her and shut the door to the family room. The computer was on, and she logged onto IM, hoping Max was around. He was online, as always.

E: my mom's making me nuts.

M: Candied walnuts?? I like candied walnuts.

E: ha. she's giving me massive prom pressure.

M: Did u tell her about the crashing?

E: um. no.

M: Should I suggest she go 2 the mall on Sat night 2 snap some pics of u and Neil?

E: !!!!!! u better not!

M: R u ok?

E: yeah. a little annoyed. but i know she's just really into prom.

M: So r u.

E: which is why i don't want her 2 remind me every 4 secs that i don't have a date.

M: U will have a date. Soon enough.

E: i hope so. ready 4 sat?

M: Yup. My tux is pressed, my hair's been washed. I'm good 2 go.

E: great. clean hair's a plus.

M: Agreed. ... r u gonna be ok?

E: yeah. have a good night, k, max?

M: U 2. Prom #1 here we come!

Five

Emily clutched the bottom of her dress in her fist, fabric pulled taut over the back of her thighs. She knew that when she released the ball of shimmery pink satin, it would be wrinkled and sweaty. She didn't care.

It was the first Saturday of prom season, and she was wiped. So far, crashing proms wasn't easy—particularly since Emily was attempting to attend her first two proms in the same building at exactly the same time.

She had just left date number one—Neil—right outside the doors of Marshall's prom, excusing herself to go to the bathroom. In reality, she was running off to prom number two.

It had taken *way* longer than Emily had

expected to get from the mall to Neil's prom. They had met up with a bunch of Neil's guy friends for a romantic preprom meal at Taco Bell, then the whole group went back to someone's house for pictures.

Emily had stood to the side as the parents—who were all gathered together at one house—took picture after picture of the guys hamming it up and trying to look manly. Except for a few choice "babe" remarks, they mostly ignored Emily. She chalked it up to their insecurity.

It felt like hours later when they finally piled into a big van and got a ride to the convention center from one of the dads. Emily had promised to meet Max at eight thirty outside Park's prom, and as they pulled into the parking lot of the convention center, she felt like it was already midnight. She felt bad for thinking it, but spending time with Neil and his friends made time drag more slowly than a really bad civics class. Emily was pretty sure she was late.

As soon as they stepped inside the convention center, Emily excused herself—agreeing to meet Neil outside the Marshall prom doors in fifteen minutes—and ran through the halls of the city convention center to find Max. She was a little scared Max would think she had already been there and would leave or try to get in himself. Patience wasn't one of his strengths.

Emily slowed to a walk as she came around the corner into the main hall of the convention center. The entrance to Park's prom was at the top of a long escalator. She rode up, searching for Max in the crowd gathered near the main doors. She couldn't find him, but Emily was instantly aware of the ticket takers guarding the only entrance to the ballroom. She and Max would need to be creative if they had any hope of getting in.

Across the hall, Emily noticed a guy who looked vaguely familiar. *Uh-oh*, she thought, ducking her head. It was one of the guys from the Foot Locker in the mall—he knew she didn't go to Park. Slipping behind a pillar, Emily gave herself a second to breathe.

"Can I help you?" A perky-voiced brunette appeared in Emily's periphery. The bouncy hair and flushed cherub cheeks belonged to a short, well-endowed girl who was squeezed into a sequined silver dress. It looked like the dress was holding all her body parts in, and if someone snipped the back, everything would pop out. "Everything okay back here?"

"Yeah," Emily said, smiling back. "Okay."

"Are you looking for someone?" There was a glint of something—suspicion, recognition, kindness?—in her eyes. "Because I can help you. I'm Ally, by the way." She laughed. "But you knew that."

Emily nodded. She needed to get out of there. It seemed like Max hadn't yet arrived, and she needed to get back to Neil. "Uh—" she stuttered. "Time?" she asked meekly. It was as though she suddenly couldn't form full sentences.

"What time is it?" Ally expanded the question for Emily. "Eight thirty. Time to vote for prom queen!"

"Uh-huh." Emily slipped past Ally and made a hasty retreat back down the escalator. She was right on time, and it looked like Max was late. She would have to come back again in a few minutes and just hope Max would wait nicely until she got back. Neil would surely think something strange was going on if she wasn't back soon.

As promised, Neil was standing just outside the Marshall prom doors waiting. She felt a twinge of guilt for double-dating behind his back. But the guilt melted away as soon as she stepped inside the doors to the prom and took one lap around the perimeter with Neil. The prom was scary, to say the least. And Neil? Not charming.

There were only eighty people at the event, and not a single one even remotely resembled her hot crush. Everyone was grinding on the dance floor, and the sweat from the perfumed bodies mingled with the smell of catered pork egg rolls to create a funky, floral mist in the air.

Emily wanted to vomit.

Neil paraded Emily around the small, cramped ballroom, stopping periodically to greet one or another of his acquaintances. While he and his friends high-fived and swapped postprom party plans, Emily looked around the room for Ethan.

He was definitely nowhere in sight.

Emily was itching to escape, eager to meet up with Max. But Neil had a firm grip on her arm, and she knew she couldn't use the bathroom excuse again this soon. She spotted a punch table across the dance floor and vowed to drink as many cups as were necessary to make it obvious to everyone that she really *ought* to go to the bathroom. "Hey, Neil," she said, tugging the arm of his tux. "Do you want a glass of punch?"

Neil smirked and said, "Sure." He looked around at his friends, then continued, "But don't you think we should get to know each other a little better first?" He laughed, slapping hands with one of his friends. Emily ignored the innuendo—she wasn't sure how his comment was even remotely relevant or appropriate to the question.

"Okay, Neil." She strolled across the room and filled two big glasses full of punch. She quickly took another look around for Ethan, then returned to Neil and his friends. She caught the tail end of their conversation as she returned to the outside of their circle.

". . . Emily's hot, isn't she?" one of Neil's friends was asking. Emily blushed—compliments were always appreciated, even from this crowd.

Neil's back was turned, so he couldn't see Emily approaching when he said, "Oh, yeah. I'm in there." Then he turned to gesture to Emily. When he saw her standing behind him, he grabbed his glass out of her hand, put it on a table, and led her to the dance floor.

She quickly downed her glass of punch and followed Neil's lead. After a few deliberately not-too-close slow dances, she grabbed another drink.

"Thirsty?" Neil asked, wagging his eyebrows.

Emily smiled thinly and nodded. "Mm-hmm."

"I know how to quench your thirst." Neil laughed at his grotesque line as he turned toward another group of friends. Emily gagged and rolled her eyes before following him. She got to his side just in time to hear her prom date announcing, "Neil's the man. This chick is totally into me!" while not-so-subtly pointing to Emily. She pretended not to hear.

She was playing dumb. It was her survival strategy.

Four cups of punch later, Emily finally managed to escape Neil's sweaty embrace, and she ran from the Great Lakes Ballroom to Hall A (with a bathroom break on the way), where Park's prom was already in full swing.

When she arrived, Max was standing with his back facing her, looking mighty fine in his dad's tails.

"Hey, you." Emily huffed. She was out of breath and suspected she was emanating the stench of egg rolls.

Max turned. "You look nice. Cute corsage."

Emily glanced down. She had managed to forget she was wearing the corsage Neil had given her. It was a bouquet of brightly dyed carnations, and itched her wrist like crazy. When Max pointed to it, she scratched at the raw skin on her wrist and peeled the cheap elastic and flowers from her arm. She tossed it into a nearby garbage can and reminded herself to come up with an excuse for its disappearance when she returned to Neil.

"Have you been here long?" she asked. She carefully studied the couples entering and leaving the Hall, formulating a plan. "I came earlier, but you weren't here yet. Then I couldn't get away."

"Maybe half an hour. No biggie."

Emily spotted a group of several couples drunkenly making their way up the escalator toward the hall. She linked arms with

Max and approached the group as they boisterously piled off the escalator. Emily plastered a smile on her face and approached one of the girls in the group, draping her in a huge hug.

"Heeeeey!" she said, giggling. "You look soooooo cute!" The girl gave Emily a weird look. Emily continued. "Did you guys go to Monaco's for dinner? Yum."

Emily had now attracted the attention of another girl in the group. Luckily this girl was piss drunk and easily fooled. She pushed past her date and the first girl and slurred, "Nuh-uh. We went to Kelly's." She leaned in to Emily, whispering conspiratorially. "*So* good. But I maybe had a teensy-eensy bit too much champagne in the limo. Shhhhhh." She stumbled, then righted herself again. "You're in my history class, right?"

"Yeah," Emily responded. "What's your name again?"

Drunk girl linked arms with Emily and Max. "Claudia!" Emily and Max blended into the middle of the group of Claudia and her drunken buddies—none of whom, except Claudia, had really noticed Emily or Max—and weaved past the teachers into the prom.

They were in.

Inside, it was insanity. Since prom had already been cooking for more than an hour, the dance floor was packed. The Black Eyed Peas were pumping from the speakers onstage, and there were several girls on the dance floor whose already too-short and too-tight skirts were now riding dangerously close to the butt-cheek line. A line of desperate-looking guys stood nearby, gawking and smiling at one another.

Emily held Max's arm tightly. She could feel him shaking with laughter through the sleeve of his tux. She nudged him in the ribs to remind him that they needed to get their job done before pissing anyone off.

Glancing around the ballroom, Emily immediately gathered that the Park prom theme was Under the Sea. Streamers and crepe paper had been hung over the ceiling tiles, creating the illusion of waves and water. The streamers covered the air-conditioning vents, trapping the cool air behind crystal blue waves. As a result, under the sea felt a lot like a sauna.

There were tiny fish hanging from all the chairs, and clusters of shells were spread over the tablecloths. The buffet table was encased in a giant mermaid tail; a chocolate fountain erupted from the center. It looked like the mermaid was hemorrhaging mud.

Most of the tables had been pushed to the edge of the room. Emily and Max weaved in and out of them, making their way around the room. "I don't see Ethan," Emily said, squinting for a better view of the dance floor. She had glasses but refused to wear them. Her mom had gotten the frames on clearance at Dylan's, and they looked like something an evening news anchor would wear.

"What are you going to do when you find this guy?" Max asked, pulling off his jacket. His wavy hair had begun to curl in the humidity of the room, and his cheeks were flushed. "Do you just saunter up to him and say, 'Hey, I'm stalking you'?"

Emily hadn't really thought about that. She had only thought through the process of getting into the proms, but hadn't come up with a good explanation of why she was there. "Dunno. I guess I'll just have to figure that out when I find him. I'm hoping the circumstance lends itself to a reasonable explanation."

"Right," Max said. He didn't look convinced. "Care to dance?"

Emily grinned. "But of course." She led Max onto the turquoise-tiled dance floor. They squeezed into an open space next to a couple who seemed to be searching for lost treasure in each others' throats and another couple who was bickering about whether the girl's dress was "technically" green or teal. The guy seemed overly concerned.

"Bizarrely enough, I'm having fun," Max said as they started slow dancing. "You?"

"Other schools' proms are cheesy," Emily said honestly. "But yeah. It's good to get away from Neil, for sure."

"How's it going with him? No Ethan sightings, I assume?"

Emily shook her head. "No." She laughed and leaned back to look at Max. "But I enjoyed many delicious egg rolls and *a lot* of punch."

They danced silently for a few minutes—watching clusters of girls sing along to Christina Aguilera, hugging and swaying in time to the music—before Max said, "Do you remember how every time I used to spend the night at your house, we would sneak out of your basement and into my parents' kitchen to get cake?"

She nodded. "Your mom makes a mean cake."

"I *know*. I could really go for a piece of that cake right now." Max sighed. "This prom crashing thing sort of makes me feel the same way I did those nights—it's that 'we could get caught, and it's exciting' feeling. But the stakes are higher, and this time you're wearing an almost-stolen dress." He shook his head before cracking a smile. "Emily, you used to be such a nice girl. What happened?"

She smiled back. "I'm still a nice girl. And because I'm such a nice girl, I guess I should get back to Neil." Emily leaned back and rolled her eyes. "But the breath! The hair! The lame one-liners! I don't think I can go back there. No, Max, no! Don't make me go!" She raised her arm to her forehead, Scarlett O'Hara style. With the pretty gown, she was feeling almost damsel-in-distress-like.

"What if you didn't go back?" Max said, eyebrows raised. "I mean, you've already collected your corsage. You've sampled the buffet. You've conquered the prom. Would it be so awful if you just left Neil to fend for himself? Is there any reason to go back?"

Emily considered his suggestion. Max was right. Neil had his friends, and she'd completed her mission. Neil definitely wasn't "in there." So going back was just delaying the inevitable. She would eventually need to ditch Neil to get to the third prom of the night, where Sid and Charlie were waiting for them.

"I guess I could leave him there."

"That's the spirit!" Max pumped his arm in the air. They had danced over to the edge of the dance floor, and when the song ended, they broke apart. "We should probably get to Memorial's prom sometime soon anyway." He checked his watch. "It's a little after ten."

Suddenly the short, silver-gowned brunette Emily had met earlier approached them. She now wore a crown and a sash that read "Prom Queen." A trail of small, wimpy-looking girls fanned out behind her. The prom committee, Emily presumed.

Prom Queen cleared her throat and spoke. "I don't know you. And I know *everyone*."

Emily stared blankly, buying herself time to organize a response. Now that the votes were counted, it seemed Prom Queen wasn't quite as eager to make friends.

Prom Queen lifted her overplucked eyebrows. "Hmm? Who are you?" She jammed her hands into her hips. "You need to leave." Several teachers turned to stare. Prom Queen had drawn a crowd. Emily and Max needed to get out of there—now.

"You know," Emily said, directing her response to Max and pointedly ignoring Prom Queen. Her voice had taken on a combination British-Swedish-German accent. "I am very sad right now."

Max caught on. He nodded his head and said, "Yah, yah."

Prom Queen continued to stare them down.

Emily shook her head and pouted. "We have been at your school for almost one whole year, and I have come to realize . . . no one ever notices the foreign exchange students." And, turning on her heels, Emily stormed away with Max in tow.

Two proms down, seven to go. And still no Ethan.

Six

At the same time across town, Sid stood alone, swaying with the music. She couldn't stop her fingers from snapping to the beat, but she could plaster a scowl on her face, daring anyone to ask her to dance. *You can get me to prom, but you can't make me dance,* she vowed.

She glanced around the room, searching the crowded dance floor for her best friend and obvious prom addict, Charlie. She spotted him surrounded by a group of girls, all of whom were clapping and hooting, cheering him on. Charlie had broken out his signature break dancing moves and was busy impressing the prom crowd gathered in Memorial High's gymnasium.

You would never guess that an hour ago none of these people had seen Charlie before in their life. You would think Charlie was the most popular guy at Memorial High.

Sid's dress was starting to bind under her armpits. She had been wearing it since one o'clock that afternoon, and could honestly say she had never worn a dress for this many hours straight in her entire life.

She was miserable.

Checking her cell phone, Sid was relieved to see a text message envelope flashing on her screen. It had come in just two minutes before:

On our way. See you in ten. Em.

Sid smiled for the first time all night. Their plan was working.

Charlie had picked Sid up that afternoon in his ratty old Volvo. In the car, she had smeared on some glittery eye shadow for comic effect. Sid preferred to go au naturel—with the exception of her hair streak, which she had adjusted in honor of prom to match the deep blue of her dress. She had smudged a stick of lip stain across her full lips, tilting the rearview mirror toward the passenger seat to make sure she'd colored in the lines. Charlie had protested, pulling the mirror back. Sid swore at him and slouched in her seat. If she was expected to play prom crasher, she wanted to look the part. That was *at least* half the fun.

When they had arrived at Memorial High hours ago, Charlie pulled his Volvo into a spot under a dying pine tree in the parking lot. The two of them sat silently in the car for a few minutes, watching the track team running sprints behind the school. They could hear the marching band rehearsing for their spring concert on the football field in the center of the asphalt track. The trombones were out of tune.

"Ready?" Charlie asked, turning to Sid with a giant grin. He was literally bouncing in his seat. "We're on."

"I'm ready," Sid answered, significantly more subdued. She pulled her dress up and tugged it to the side—she'd only been wearing it half an hour, and already it was riding funny. "You know what gets me down when I see a band like that practic-ing?" Sid pointed to the marching band on the field as she locked her car door. One member of the drum line was chasing another around with a sweaty pair of running shorts that he had presumably taken from one of the track team members. Sid didn't want to know what the track guy was now wearing.

"There are some hotties, but their gorgeousness is wasted because they're all band freaks?" Charlie had a tendency toward prejudgment, and assumed all band members were losers. He himself was a drama geek, so go figure.

"Not what I was thinking," Sid answered. "What gets me down is the fact that that guy"—she pointed to the drum guy holding the sweaty shorts; the guy was now sniffing them—"probably has a real band he plays with, and actually gets gigs, not just the completely lame mall tea shop."

"Do you want to be in that guy's band?" Charlie's lip was in a sneer. He buttoned the top button of his tux jacket and pulled at the lapel to straighten it. "Do you want to be like that guy?"

"No, dumbass, I just want a real gig sometime. How many times do I have to send out my CDs and get rejected before someone other than 'Teas of the World' Gary hires me?"

Charlie shrugged. "Your genius has yet to be realized. You're going to be huge. If I didn't believe that, I wouldn't hang out with you. Simple as that." He pulled out two pairs of huge, dark sunglasses. "Wear these."

Sid studied him. "Oh, come on."

"For me."

She pulled the sunglasses onto her small, button nose. "Do I look fabulous?"

Charlie grinned and nodded vigorously. "Like the star that you are." They walked toward the back of the school, just up the hill from the track. The plan was that Charlie and Sid would try to sneak into Memorial High that afternoon while the doors were unlocked for track practice.

They had received this suggestion from one of the McDonald's employees at the mall, who was a junior at Memorial. He told them the school goes into lockdown mode a few hours before prom, so their only hope of getting into the prom was to actually be in the school before prom started. So while Emily and Max attended proms number one and two, Sid and Charlie were assigned the task of sneaking into Memorial High.

A tall, lean guy in short shorts jogged past them as they neared the back door of the school. He did a double take when he saw their prom wear, then offered them a high five. Charlie raised his arm to reciprocate as Sid scurried forward, catching the door track boy had just exited from with her foot.

"Nice one," Charlie said, watching the runner retreat to the field.

"Must you check everyone out?" Sid teased, grinning.

"That is so not what I meant," Charlie insisted. "I was talking about you—good catch on the door." He squeezed Sid around the middle.

She shimmied out of his grip and opened the door farther. "After you."

They both glanced around. There was no one near the back door of the school, and the track was far enough away that people couldn't really tell from that distance that they didn't belong. Quickly and quietly, they slid through the open door and into the darkened school.

Charlie whistled. "Cute smell."

"It smells like crap." Sid plugged her nose with her fingers. "This school is nasty."

The back door of the school had led them into a dark hallway that dead-ended at the gymnasium doors. The locker rooms were on either side of the hallway, their doors propped open. Charlie pulled off his sunglasses and moved toward the gym. "Just one quick peek at how the decorations are coming," he said, motioning for Sid to join him. Memorial's prom was being held in the gym that night, so they knew the prom committee and parents would be decorating all afternoon.

They crept down the hall, studying the posters that lined the wall: CARMEN CAN! VOTE MENDOZA!; PETER FOR PREZ!; VOTE ONCE, VOTE TWICE, VOTE VINCE FOR VICE!; CHRIS FOR PROM KING!

"People actually campaign for prom king?" Charlie mused, chuckling. "That's just sad."

"Admit it—you would totally do the same if it wasn't completely classless. Being prom king is your dream come true, no?"

Charlie shrugged. "I can't say it wouldn't feel fantastic. But I would never campaign. I would expect my Midwestern good looks and superhot style to speak for themselves." Charlie ran his fingers through his hair and straightened his tux again.

They were just steps away from the gym when they heard voices approaching. "In here," Sid hissed, pulling Charlie into an unlocked room. They both pressed their ears against the inside of the door, listening to the passersby.

". . . it will be worth it," Voice One was saying.

"But you don't even like her, dude," Voice Two responded.

"If I get laid, what do I care? If I pretend to be into her . . ." They couldn't hear the next line. But finally the voice boomed out, ". . . we look too hot together to not win. And when she gets that crown, she'll be like putty in my arms. Wham, bam, thank you ma'am." Voice One laughed. He sounded like a major creep.

"Chris, dude, that's harsh," Voice Two said, then laughed. Charlie and Sid could hear the slap of a high five.

Charlie turned to Sid, mouth agape. "That's the prick who's campaigning for prom king—Chris. Sounds like a good guy."

"A major jerk, more like." Sid stated the obvious.

"I'd like to see that guy taken down," Charlie mused. "A prick like that doesn't deserve prom king." He looked thoughtful. "Hmmm . . ."

"Charlie, I'm worried about the look on your face." Sid lifted her eyebrows. "What are you planning?"

"No worries, my friend," Charlie responded. "It's all good. So, what have we here?" Charlie moved beyond the door and into the room they were using as a hideout.

"Looks like the teachers' lounge."

"That it does." Charlie flopped down on the couch in the center of the room. It smelled like old hotdogs and bad breath. He quickly stood up again. "Comfy."

"Wanna just hang out in here?" Sid settled into a ratty old chair in the corner of the room. The answer key for a math exam was perched on the arm of the chair. She cast it aside, turning sideways in the chair to rest her legs over the arm.

They had found their way in. Now they just had to wait and avoid being noticed.

Going unnoticed was not one of Charlie's assets. He had a tendency to solicit attention, then milk it for all it was worth. So now, seven hours after sneaking into Memorial High and two hours into the prom, Sid stood at the edge of the gymnasium watching her best friend surrounded by his circle of new best friends.

Charlie danced and swayed, teaching the girls' basketball team (who had all arrived at prom together, dressed in identical teal dresses) how to mambo. They thought he was a god.

Not so much their boyfriends, who all stood against the folded bleachers, glowering. They were whispering to one another, and Sid was pretty sure Charlie was about to be the target of a hostile takeover. The boyfriends wanted their prom dates back.

Sid checked her watch—five minutes had passed since she got the text from Emily, so she and Max should be arriving at their meeting point in just a few minutes. Sid glanced at Charlie and decided to execute the rendezvous alone. She would give Charlie a few more minutes in the spotlight before pulling him from the mission. Emily only needed a few minutes to look for Ethan, then they could sneak out before Charlie was mauled by angry jocks.

Sid slipped out the side door of the gym, avoiding notice by any of the teacher aides. She turned a corner and hustled to the door she and Charlie had come in earlier that afternoon. She pressed the bar on the door, releasing the lock, and peeked outside. She could see Emily and Max strolling across the parking lot toward the school.

"Hey, hot stuffs!" she called, whistling at them as they walked up the hill.

Max waved. Sid pushed the door the rest of the way open. Max and Emily slipped in and Sid pulled it closed behind them. "Tiny issue," Sid announced. "You better look for Ethan quickly, because I think our cover is about to be compromised."

"What happened?" Emily asked.

"Go have a look," Sid answered cryptically.

Max and Emily followed Sid to the gym, where all three slid in through the side door. Sid had realized early in the night that all the teacher aides were congregating by the main gym entrance off the front lobby of the school, and one of the side entrances (next to the athletic director's office) was completely unguarded.

Walking into the gym, the first thing Emily noticed was a huge faux-wooden pirate ship that couples paraded over to enter and exit the prom. The boat was almost ten feet tall and was decorated with twinkling Christmas tree lights that spelled out PIRATES OF THE CARIBBEAN. She could only imagine that Orlando Bloom would be highly disappointed if he saw this sorry representation of the film.

The second thing Emily noticed was the huge mob of people in the center of the waxy dance floor. The mob seemed to be chanting something in unison, and she sort of thought it sounded like "Charlie! Charlie! Charlie!"

She moved toward the mob and realized that it was in fact what they were chanting. Her cousin was propped up on the shoulders of a bunch of girls in teal dresses, who were spinning him around the dance floor. Emily glanced over her shoulder at Sid.

"I warned you," Sid said, shrugging.

Max and Sid stood on the edge of the dance floor, keeping an eye on Charlie while Emily made a few rounds through the gym.

The gym was crowded and dim, making it hard to see faces clearly. At one point Emily thought she spotted Ethan, but as soon as the guy in question turned, she realized it was definitely not him. Emily weaved through groups of people, smiling whenever anyone looked at her curiously. Her heart sank every time she passed another Ethan-less group. Yes, it was only prom number three, but she still couldn't help but feel disappointed. She wanted to see him again.

After a few minutes of fruitless searching, she returned to Max and Sid, who were now fighting each other with plastic swords they had found on the punch table.

"Ladies and gentlemen!" An adult voice called out over a squawky mic, squealing over the din of the dance floor. "Ladies! Gentlemen! Your attention please!" A mousy woman was standing atop the pirate ship, waving her arms madly in the air. She was wearing an off-the-shoulder dress that looked dangerously close to ripping.

Parent volunteers should *not* dress up to chaperone the prom. It was wrong on so many levels.

"Folks, listen up!" mousy, off-the-shoulder mom screeched through her mic. "It's time to crown our prom king and queen!"

The noise in the gym quickly quieted down. The DJ lowered the music to a soft hum. One of the basketball girls' dates entered Charlie's circle and wrapped his arms around the waist of one of the tallest girls in the circle. "Chriiiis," she squealed, pushing him away.

Chris—the prom king candidate whose sexist comments had been haunting Sid all afternoon—was a huge, beefy sort of guy. He looked like an overripe tomato now that his face was flushed with the embarrassment of being shrugged off by his date. He chuckled to mask the awkward moment, then more loosely draped an arm over his date's shoulder. She pointedly ignored him, but didn't push him away.

Charlie's face was flushed and shiny from dancing. He hugged all the teal girls before heading across the gym floor to join his friends near the punch table. Emily and Max greeted him, then all four stood on the side of the gym, listening to the parent chaperone drone on and on about what a great four years it had been, blah, blah, blah, and how she was so proud of everyone for their accomplishments. She looked like she was primed for a good, long cry.

"Now the moment you've all been waiting for," she said happily. "The crowning of this year's prom queen and king!" She motioned to one of the teacher aides, who was wearing a pirate hat. The teacher aide stepped forward and held up a cardboard circle with a red arrow stuck to it.

"What the hell?" Sid muttered to Emily under her breath.

"As always," the teacher aide shouted over the crowd, "the votes will be tabulated by our patented applause meter."

"Oh, come on," Emily murmured back. "This has to be a joke."

Max was shaking with laughter. "Too good to be true," he concluded.

The parent chaperone tapped her mic with three loud thumps to quiet the crowd. "Kids. Keep it down." She held up a clipboard. "Nominations have been collected all evening by Frances, your favorite cafeteria manager. Thank you, Frances." Mousy mom nodded to a maybe-man-maybe-woman near the door. She or he nodded back. "The nominations for this year's prom queen are: Shiloh, Jordan, and Britney C."

Three of the teal girls, including Chris's date, squealed and bounced with glee.

"By a show of applause, who would like to see Shiloh crowned?" A handful of people cheered and clapped. The teacher holding the applause meter moved the arrow to the center of the dial. A perky blond girl bowed her head and smiled.

"Jordan?" The room exploded with applause and hoots. The applause meter was adjusted so the arrow was almost all the way at the other side of the dial. Chris grabbed his slender, willowy date and planted a kiss on her mouth. She pushed him off.

"And Britney?" A slightly less exuberant roar came from the crowd, including a few of the boyfriends who were leaning against the bleachers. The arrow was moved to the middle of the dial.

"Jordan, congratulations!" The mom squealed with delight as Jordan ran toward Charlie.

Charlie gave her a huge hug and shouted, "You go, girl! Get your crown!" Jordan walked toward the pirate ship and climbed the plank. She was handed a crown and a bouquet of lilies.

"Congratulations, Jordan," mousy mom repeated earnestly. "And now, we'll find out who will be your king. The nominations for this year's prom king are"—she consulted her clipboard—"Shawn, Chris, and Charlie!"

Charlie looked around the room. Chris was shaking hands with another guy, but there didn't seem to be a third guy in the room.

"Is that me?" he turned to Emily, grinning.

Emily shrugged. "Sort of looks that way, doesn't it?"

The teal girls all ran toward Charlie and surrounded him with hugs and cheers.

Chris did *not* look happy.

"Can I hear a round of applause for those of you who want to see Shawn crowned as your king?" A group of abnormally tall guys cheered and whooped—*Shawn must be a basketball player,* Emily surmised.

"And Chris?" All the guys who were slumped along the bleachers shouted and stomped. Chris bowed.

"Charlie?" The teal girls screamed and shouted and raised their fists in the air. So did half the other people in the room. The cardboard applause meter said it all—Charlie was the new Memorial High Prom King.

Charlie jogged toward the pirate ship, waving and grinning ear to ear. He collected his plastic-and-rhinestone crown and gave Jordan a quick hug. The two of them promenaded across the pirate ship together, waving at the crowd below. Everyone was cheering as "You're Beautiful" began to play in the background. Charlie and Jordan descended to the gym floor and mamboed through their inaugural dance.

It wasn't until Charlie dipped his queen at the end of the song that he noticed the posse of large, imposing jocks (led by Chris) approaching the dance floor.

Luckily Sid noticed the pack at the same time and was able to quickly alert Emily and Max. The three of them ran together toward the dance floor, grabbing Charlie by the arms, then ran as fast as they could around the pirate ship, through the halls, and out the school's back door. They didn't stop running until they got to Charlie's Volvo in the parking lot.

"Get in," Emily panted. "We can come back for Max's car!"

All four jumped in the Volvo and erupted in a fit of laughter. As Charlie drove out of the lot, they could see Chris and his gang emerging from the school's front doors. Charlie pulled his crown off his head and waved it out the window at Chris. "I'll take care of the crown! You take care of your girl!" he called, then replaced it on his head and sped off toward the freeway.

Charlie was still wearing the crown later that night in a corner booth at Burrito Jack's. "My greatest goal in life has been accomplished," he declared, rubbing his thumb over the crown's rhinestones. "I am the prom king!"

"It's not even your own school," Sid said, dunking a chip in salsa. "Does that count?"

"Of course it counts," Emily answered for her cousin. "I say it's worth double *because* it's not your school."

"Agreed," Max said, pouring a packet of sugar into his glass of water.

Charlie sighed and leaned back into the puffy booth. "I wish Marco could have been there to see me tonight." Charlie was smiling, but Emily could tell he really missed his boyfriend. "Man, I would have loved to see the look on his face. Me as prom king? He'll never believe it."

Sid was first to respond. "He'll believe it," she said simply. She was drawing little dragons on the paper tablecloth with a purple crayon. She looked up from her art to say, "He does know you, right? It's not as if this is so unexpected."

"But it wasn't even my own prom." He turned to Sid. "What if I win prom king at South and he's not there?"

"Is it desirable to win?" Sid scoffed. She drew horns on her creation.

"Uh." Charlie widened his eyes. "Yeah.

Why are you and Marco both so negative about prom? Because my best friend and my boyfriend are both ditching me, I'm stuck going to our prom with Natasha Fine." He paused. Charlie had earlier that week agreed to go to South's prom with one of his drama club leading ladies. "Admittedly, Natasha Fine dresses well and is really fun, but still . . . not Marco."

"Charlie," Emily interrupted, "does Marco know you want him to go? Have you asked him?" She reached across the table to draw a green flame coming out of Sid's dragon's mouth.

"Not as such."

"Then it's your own damn fault," Sid retorted.

"Too late now, isn't it?" Charlie responded snippily. "I'm going with Natasha, and we will look *fine*." He faux-pouted. "Marco's payback will be my detailed phone account of each and every prom. Every last, cheesy detail. He will learn to *love* prom."

Through her teeth, Sid jokingly muttered, "And my payback is that I get to go to prom over and over and over again with you people."

Max had been mostly silent since they

had left Memorial, but broke in suddenly. "You know, tonight gave me an idea."

The other three looked at him, waiting.

"We have four proms left to crash, plus our own, right?" Emily nodded yes. "How would you guys feel about me chronicling our prom crashing for an article? I think I could definitely sell this somewhere. I'll make you all sound much prettier and funnier than you actually are, of course."

"Oh, thanks," Emily said sarcastically, leaning against her best friend. "But seriously, go for it. It could be a good story. Oddly enough, prom crashing is more normal than your usual pieces, so maybe it stands a chance." Sid nodded her agreement.

Charlie grinned. "Will you include the part about me winning prom king?" he asked. "Because I did! I won prom king!"

Sid rolled her eyes, leaning her head on the table. "I get the feeling we might be hearing about this *forever*."

"So after tonight, we have four proms to go," Emily said. She had a feeling things would be getting a lot more complicated—their first night of crashing had been relatively easy.

"Are you still excited about finding this guy?" Sid asked.

"Mmm-hmm. If it's possible, I think I'm actually more excited about my own prom now that I've been to these other bizarre proms."

"You know"—Max grinned, wiggling his eyebrows—"I'm still willing to be your backup date for our prom."

Emily and Max had agreed years ago to go together if neither of them could find a real date. But Emily always thought going to prom just for the sake of going to prom was a little depressing. She really wanted her nice, long good-night kiss from a sexy tuxedoed date. Max just wasn't going to give her that.

"Um, yeah." Emily nodded slowly. "I think I'll keep holding out for the real thing."

Max shrugged. "Fine. The offer's out there. . . ."

Sid and Charlie exchanged a look.

"What?" Emily demanded. Sid just stared back at her.

"That just came out a little harsh, maybe," Max responded, clearly a little hurt. "I'm not *that* bad."

"You know what I mean, right?" Emily looked at him, concerned. She hadn't meant for her comment to be construed as rude or insulting—just honest.

"Of course. No hurt feelings." Max took a sip of his sugary water and smiled. "You know I don't want to go to prom anyway, so whatever."

"For sure?" Emily inquired again. Now she was worried. He was acting like they hadn't talked about this a million times. She *knew* how Max felt about prom.

"For sure," Max echoed. But suddenly Emily wasn't so sure she believed him.

Seven

"Big news! F—flaming good news!" Sid came barreling into the Leaf Lounge the next Tuesday night while Emily was sitting at the counter, sharing a muffin with Frank. He had bought a chocolate-chunk muffin, making Emily happier than ever when he offered—as always—to share it.

"She's a little cutie, isn't she?" Frank asked Emily under his breath while Sid scooted a stool up to the counter.

"Don't let her hear you say that," Emily warned. "She's not big on little compliments."

"What am I not big on?" Sid asked. "Where's Charlie?"

"In back." Emily ignored her first question. "What's up?"

Charlie poked his head around the door of the back room, iPod buds in his ears. "Sidney! My knight in shining armor!" He had been "sorting inventory" for the past two hours and came flying out of the back room now, declaring that he "needed a break." Said break conveniently coincided with Sid's arrival.

Sid leaned over the counter to grab a clean mug from the dish rack. She filled it with coffee from the thermos next to the register. "Help yourself," Emily said. "Really."

Frank chuckled to himself, murmuring, "What a cutie. Such moxie."

Sid pointedly ignored Frank, then blurted out, "I got a gig!"

"What's a gig?" Frank asked Emily. "A horse?" He turned to Sid. "You got a horse?"

Emily shook her head at Frank and held a finger to her lips. "Where? When are you playing? I assume we can come, right?"

"That's the crazy part. It's this Saturday!" She drumrolled her hands on the countertop. "At the Ridley Prep prom after-party!"

Ridley Prep was one of the smallest schools in the area, with only about forty seniors. So far, the only thing Emily knew about the Ridley prom was that the highlight of the night was always the after-party. Everyone went to the same party, and it was usually held at a downtown hot spot. Ridley Prep was known around town for its ultracool hipster reputation, and Emily and Charlie had been trying to figure out the best way in.

Charlie climbed up on the counter and leaned over to give Sid a big hug. "That's so great, babe!"

Frank stood up from his stool, patting Sid on the shoulder. "Good luck with your 'gig.'" He chuckled, making quotes in the air. "Gig," he muttered as he strolled out the front door.

"Wow, Sid, that's incredible," Emily said. "How did they find you?"

"The president of their student council heard my music on MySpace. He IMed me a few days ago, I sent him a CD, and I guess he must have liked it. They have a couple of bands lined up, and I'm second to go on."

"Can we come? Please please please please please!" Charlie hopped down from the counter.

"I was thinking I do sort of need stage-hands, right?" Sid asked, winking. "I could use some help with setup, sound checks, that sort of thing. I think we can figure out a way to get you guys in. So prom number five is taken care of."

"That's fantastic." Emily smiled happily. "You have your first real, live, non–Leaf Lounge gig. I'm so impressed."

"Thanks." Sid raked her fingers through her short, choppy hair. "Aw, shucks, now you're embarrassing me."

A customer came through the front of the coffee shop. Charlie quickly grabbed a dish towel and pretended to be drying mugs. He looked at Emily, nodding his head in the direction of the customer at the front counter. She sighed and moved forward to take the person's order.

After preparing a large latte, she turned back to the side counter where Sid was sitting. Charlie was squatting in a corner under the counter, hiding. "You will do anything and everything to get out of work, won't you?" She pushed him gently, causing him to lose his balance and topple onto the nasty floor.

He flicked a dishtowel at her butt, then

stood up to say, "So if we have an in at prom number five, we just need to figure out number four and we'll be all set for this weekend. My tux is clean, I'm in good health, it's all good. Now we just need to get into Jefferson."

"That's the problem—we have to get into Jefferson." Thomas Jefferson's prom was to be held that Friday night at the Legends Ballroom, and Jefferson's school events were famously well guarded. Emily knew they wouldn't be able to sneak in. Joey Frank, a movie star who was originally from one of the nearby suburbs, was a senior at Thomas Jefferson (though most of his course work was done via independent study from L.A.). Apparently he had invited his current costar, Simone Rocha, to be his prom date. Everyone was desperate to get into the school's prom to catch a glimpse of the Hollywood couple in action.

Thomas Jefferson had scheduled their prom for Friday night, rather than Saturday, to better accommodate Joey's filming schedule. (He was due back in L.A. on Saturday afternoon for reshoots.) Which meant Emily and her friends could focus on one prom each night that weekend—if they could get into Friday night's event.

"What if we try the sneak-in-before-prom thing again?" Charlie suggested.

Emily shook her head. "Not gonna happen. The Legends Ballroom opens when the caterers and staff arrive for the event. There's no side entrance—we'll be way too obvious."

"I could try to have one of those crazy *Charlie's Angels* masks made that would turn me into Joey Frank. I'm sure they won't fault Joey for 'forgetting' his ticket."

"Yeah, no problem, Charlie," Emily responded. "I'm sure those are easy to come by. We could try to rappel in—hook up a wire that would string us down from the roof and through a window? That would be fun."

Charlie laughed. "Oh, and that's so much more reasonable than one of those masks?"

Sid suddenly knocked her palm against the counter. "I have an idea."

Charlie and Emily stared at her, waiting.

"Remember my cousin Sam?" Sid turned to Charlie expectantly.

"Floss-in-public Sam?"

"Yes, Charlie, Sam is the cousin who flossed his teeth while you were in the car. I know it was gross—get over it. Anyway,

Sam's friend Jeremy has asked me out, like, a hundred times. And I think he goes to Thomas Jefferson. I would *maybe* be willing to try to get an invite to his prom. But there would be a condition, obviously."

Emily nodded. "Of course. What is it?" Sid's upcoming gig had made her overly generous. The old Sid would never have volunteered to ask out someone she'd already rejected. That was *not* her style.

"You would have to double with me, Em. If I can get us dates, are you in?"

"Of course."

"Let me see what I can do."

Emily spent half her lunch period the next day staring at Gina Morgenthal's table in the cafeteria. Gina Morgenthal had been one of Emily's best friends from fourth through eighth grade, but as soon as they'd hit high school, Gina had gone all loud and cheerleadery, and they hadn't really spoken since. Emily was still slightly fascinated by her, though, and had always wondered what had happened to break them apart.

It wasn't like Emily was totally out of the in crowd. But she knew she didn't fit into Gina's new world, with its wedged sandals and—if she were being honest—hoochy shirts.

That day, Gina had laid eleven *Seventeen* magazine spreads out on her lunch table, with a selection of prom dresses for her friends to admire and comment on. They were all actually sighing over a lavender satin slip dress.

"Jealous?" Max asked from across the table. He had a bite of pizza in his mouth, a piece of which slipped out when he spoke. He plucked the piece of crust off his shirt and popped it onto his tray. He smiled, which made little dimples appear in his cheeks. His smiles were contagious.

"Jealous about what?" she asked, grabbing his pizza from his plate and taking a bite off the side he hadn't eaten off yet. Her salad tasted like yard waste, and she had left it untouched on the edge of the table since three minutes into their lunch period.

"Prom. Our prom." Max gestured to Gina and her friends, huddled around the magazine clippings across the room.

"No. Why should I be?" A defensive tone crept into her voice. "I have two weekends of proms to crash before our prom—so there's still a chance I might find my date."

Max raised his hands in a surrender motion. "Sheesh. I was just asking because you've been staring at Gina Morgenthal's virtual prom dress buffet for the last ten minutes. It just seems like you're a little . . . well, jealous."

Emily groaned, relaxing her forehead onto her fists on the table. "I don't know why I'm staring. Yeah, I guess you're right. I'm a little bummed about prom. I guess I always thought I'd be dating someone who would pick me up in a limo and meet my parents and take pictures, and we'd dance and laugh and maybe kiss next to the buffet table."

"A kiss next to the buffet table?" Max asked, dimples appearing again. "Sounds romantic."

"You know what I mean. I just thought things would be different."

Max reached across the table and set the rest of his pizza on Emily's tray. "Will cold mystery-meat pizza help?"

Emily lifted her head and faux-pouted. "Yes, I think it will. Thank you." She took a bite out of the slice of pizza, but set it down again as Lauren Ellstrom—student council president and certified hottie—

walked past their table. She watched Max's gaze shift from her pizza to Lauren's approaching boobs. Emily was embarrassed for him. It was fully obvious.

Just as Emily opened her mouth to comment on his less-than-subtle staring, Lauren stopped short, just steps from their table. "Hey, Max," Lauren cooed. Emily was the one staring now. *When did my best friend become friends with* Lauren?

"Hey, Lauren." Max flushed red. "Thanks again for last week."

"No problemo, babe. Thank you for asking me. It was fun hanging out with you."

"You too," Max smiled, dimpling again. Emily got a sick feeling in her stomach. *Lauren?*

"Hey," Lauren said, leaning in toward Max, "do you have a date for prom yet?"

"Prom? No." Max was acting goofy. Emily wanted to slap him.

"Reeeeally?" Lauren smiled broadly. "Good to know." She smiled at both Emily and Max, then retreated to her own table.

Emily turned to Max, who was fiddling with a crumble of pizza crust on his tray. "What was that all about?"

"Lauren?" Max asked, still fiddling.

"Nothing. She just helped me with a story idea. It was fun. She's cool."

Emily nodded. But watching Max smile as he pushed crumbs around his tray, she couldn't stop a jealous, possessive sort of feeling from creeping from her stomach into her throat. She had never had to deal with Max dating, or even being interested in anyone—and she wasn't sure she was ready to start. She didn't like to share.

The sound of her ring tone broke through her jealousy, relieving her of having to think about why she was feeling the way she was feeling. She grabbed her phone out of her pocket. A text message was flashing on her screen. It was from Sid:

We're in at Jefferson. You're going with a guy named Danny. Call me asap, there's a catch.

"Hey, it's Emily Bronson." Silence hung on the other side of the phone. During a superquick call between sixth and seventh period, Sid had given Emily the name and number of her Friday prom date, and told her she should make nice and call him. But now Emily was thinking maybe Sid had given her the wrong number. Emily kept talking. "Your prom date? Sidney Martinez's friend?"

"Greetings, Emily Bronson." Silence.

Okaaaay, Emily thought, raising her eyebrows. Out loud she said, "How are you, Danny?"

"Well, Emily Bronson. I'm doing well." More silence.

"Greeeeat. So, I just wanted to call and figure out our plan for Friday. I was thinking we would just maybe meet up at the ballroom?"

"Think again, Emily Bronson." *Okay, freak,* Emily thought. *You're starting to creep me out.*

"No?" she asked. "Do you need me to pick you up?"

"In a sense," Danny said, getting weirder by the minute. If this guy didn't know Sid's cousin, she would swear he was psycho. Thank God they were doubling. "You'll need to come to my house to get ready and have our portraits done."

"Oh, pictures," Emily said, groaning.

"No, Emily Bronson." Danny's diction was frighteningly crisp. "Portraits, not pictures."

"Uh-huh, yeah." Emily wasn't sure this date was going to be worth it. She wrapped up the conversation as quickly as she could, getting Danny's address and agreeing to meet him at his house at six on Friday. "By the way, I'm wearing pink." Emily figured she should throw him a bone. Danny didn't sound like they type of guy who would be great at picking out a corsage.

"We'll see about that, Emily Bronson," Danny said, then Emily heard a click. Their conversation was over.

Eight

Emily's suspicions were confirmed when she turned up at Danny's house that Friday night. She had made a mistake agreeing to this date. The first warning sign was the bust of Shakespeare sitting on one of the branches of the apple tree in Danny's front yard.

The second was the garden gnome collection. Garden gnomes had always freaked her out.

The third warning sign—the one that was accompanied by whistles and bells and sirens—came when she knocked on the door and met Danny live and in person. She should have run screaming as soon as she'd met her date, but she politely stuck around.

She figured she couldn't really leave before Sid got there—she wouldn't leave her friend to go it alone. And she *did* want to get into Jefferson's prom. It could be Ethan's school.

If nothing else, based on Danny's first impression, this stood to be the most amusing crashing target yet. Sid was right—there was definitely a "catch."

The catch was that Danny intended to go to prom dressed in a white wig and tails. For real. Not as a joke. He looked just like a teenage George Washington.

In their first five minutes together, Emily learned that Danny was the president of Thomas Jefferson's drama club and, because he apparently took his thespian reputation very seriously, felt the need to show up at prom in full costume.

Emily was mortified.

But even though things seemed bad when she met Danny and saw his outfit—and realized she would be going to prom with *that* guy, the one everyone else would be whispering about—things quickly spiraled into much worse. Danny expected his date—Emily—to coordinate her look with his. He had rented a matching costume for her.

The tag on the rental bag said "Victorian

Lady." She wanted to crawl under one of the garden gnomes in the yard and hide. It was that bad.

Sid arrived, date in tow, at Danny's house while Emily was in Danny's upstairs bathroom changing. Emily had protested and fought and refused to put on the costume, but Danny's heart was set on going to prom as one half of a thespian couple. He told Emily that if she refused the "Victorian Lady" costume, she could forget about going to the prom. He then crossed his arms and tapped his foot.

She was left very little choice.

When Emily came gliding down the stairs in all her Victorian glory, Danny's parents whistled. Sid, who stood just to the side of the front door, choked back a laugh.

"Nice . . . ," she sputtered out. Emily cut her off with a loud cough.

"You," Danny declared as Emily pulled up her skirts around her ankles to descend the last few steps, "look *regal*."

"Great," Emily muttered. "Can we just go now?"

"Portraits! Portraits!" Danny's mom cried, pulling her camera off the front hall table.

"Yeah, Emily." Sid smiled politely. "Don't

forget about pictures. We all want to remember this night."

"I'm not so worried," Emily said, smiling back at her friend. "I think this night may dig itself into my memory book *somehow*."

Sorry, Sid mouthed as Emily was pulled into Danny's living room for pictures.

Emily shook her head in response and shrugged. Out loud she said, "I can handle it."

She obligingly trudged to the front of the fireplace, where Danny had assembled an old wooden chair and a musket. He motioned for her to sit, while he stood behind her, one hand on her shoulder, the other holding the musket. She pursed her lips, posing in the most "regal" style she could muster. Danny beamed behind her.

Emily knew the subdued snickering was coming from Sid, who stood in the door of the living room next to her shy—but otherwise normal—date, Jeremy. Emily gave herself up to the moment, posing and preening in her costume to the best of her ability. Soon the photos were over, and Danny, whose boundless energy was somewhat startling, flounced over to the window.

Danny pulled a curtain aside and glanced outside. He turned back to address Emily,

Sid and her date, and his parents. His face was flushed. "It's here!"

"What's here?" Emily asked, praying that his answer would be "An alien ship to take me away." Danny ignored her question and led them all outside. At the end of Danny's long driveway, parked between two garden gnomes, was a horse-drawn carriage.

"Everybody in!" he cried. "Action!"

Looking at each other, Sid and Emily couldn't stop themselves from cracking up. Emily shook with laughter, her chest pressing against confines of her corset. Sid hopped onto the seat next to Emily's and shouted, "Giiiiiiddy-up!"

As they trotted away from Danny's parents' house, Emily whispered to Sidney the question she'd been turning over in her mind: "What do I do if Ethan *is* at this prom?"

Sid linked arms with Emily and whispered back, "Let's just hope it doesn't come to that. Because honestly, it might be best if you *don't* reintroduce yourself while wearing a corset."

By the time the horse-drawn carriage delivered them to the front door of the Legends Ballroom—a long, chilly forty-five minutes after leaving Danny's house—Emily had numbed to the idea that she might run into Ethan in full costume.

If possible, she wouldn't let it happen. But if she did spot him, she would simply avoid him while somehow finding out his last name. Then she could track him down later.

Emily was a do-something-daring-and-unexpected kind of girl, like streaking through a cow field on a cold, snowy night in nothing but winter boots; or breaking into the condemned Elk Park Elementary school just for the thrill of it; or crashing proms to find a guy. But wearing a Victorian gown to a prom with three hundred attendees was definitely taking things one step further. This wasn't adventurous . . . it was just plain embarrassing.

She stepped out of the carriage after Danny and followed her date into the building amid stares and whispers. Danny puffed up his chest, adjusted his white wig, and pulled his tickets and school ID from his wallet. Clearly Danny was pretty comfortable in his own skin. He wasn't even reacting to the stares. Emily couldn't help but admire his unwavering self-confidence.

After passing security—which included

a metal detector (Danny had to hand over his cane) and a swift pat down (it took two female guards to lift all of Emily's skirts to check for contraband)—Danny swept the door of the ballroom open for Emily, leading her into the crowded prom.

She and Sid were in.

The first thing Emily saw when she stepped into the room was the movie star and his date. Joey and Simone were crouched at a table near the dance floor, surrounded by teachers and parents. The students at Thomas Jefferson were mostly leaving them alone, but the same couldn't be said for the parents, who were all smiling at them and leaning in to hear Joey and Simone's conversation. Joey gestured to one of his friends, who shimmied across the dance floor to greet him. Joey whispered a few quick words in his friend's ear, then the friend shouted to some unseen person across the room, "Hey, Morris, how's that beer bong?"

All the parents and teachers quickly hurried off in the direction of the supposed infraction. Joey gave his buddy a quick high five to thank him for getting rid of the chaperone huddle.

Danny, who had noticed Emily staring

at Joey, scoffed. "That guy's a total fake," he declared, not even remotely. concerned about who might hear him.

"Pardon?" Emily said, trying to stay in character. She had developed a character accent and language during their carriage ride to the ballroom. As she had told Sid, it helped make the bizarre situation a little more amusing for her.

"That guy—Joey." Danny gestured to Danny and Simone. "He's a terrible actor. He didn't even make the chorus in our sophomore year musical. He can't sing, dance, or act. He just looks pretty."

"I don't think he's that bad." Emily shrugged. "I really liked *The Hunt*."

"Of course you did. Every girl loves Joey Frank." Danny rolled his eyes. "I assume you want an introduction?"

"To Joey?"

Danny nodded. "Isn't that the reason you wanted to come to my prom? I'm not stupid, you know. I know you just wanted an in so you could meet 'the movie star.'" He made finger quotes and waved casually in Danny's directly. "Come on, I'll introduce you."

"No," Emily said, shaking her head. "I'm not at all interested in meeting Joey."

"Ohhhh," Danny said, nodding slowly. "You're obsessed with Simone, huh? That's cool. I don't know her, though."

"Danny, I'm not interested in meeting either of them."

"Then why are you here?"

Emily considered for a moment, and realized it wouldn't hurt if she let Danny in on their plan. He actually seemed pretty cool now that she was getting used to him, and if he was okay with the fact that she had, presumably, just come as his date to meet Joey Frank, how mad could he be that she had a different mission? "I'm here to find a guy," she said finally. She glanced across the room and saw Sid and Jeremy chatting at a table on the edge of the dance floor. Sid looked relatively content.

Danny laughed. "Don't tell me you're a serial promist." He laughed harder. "Do you use proms as, like, an alternative to online dating or something?"

"No! It's not like that!" Now Emily was laughing as she tried to defend herself. She filled Danny in on how she had met Ethan, and the prom crashing mission.

"So how many proms have you been to?" he asked when she had finished.

"This is number four."

"Four? You've been to four proms?" Danny whistled. "I'm impressed. How many do you have left?"

"After tonight, we have three left to crash."

"Wow. I wish I'd known this was the reason you wanted to come to prom with me," Danny said. "I probably would have scaled back the costume stuff."

Emily groaned. "Seriously? Did you make me dress like this just to punish me for using you to get to Joey and Simone?"

"A little," Danny confessed. "I've always wanted to come to prom in costume, though, so it worked out pretty well for me. It's always fun to surprise and shock people—everyone's so uptight at this school, I shake it up by doing things differently. But I guess I did put a little extra act on just to see how bad you wanted to be here. You passed the test." He smiled sheepishly.

"I guess I did." Emily looked down at her gown and grinned again. "You know what, Danny? I'm glad I came—even the ridiculous costume isn't so bad. You're right about people being uptight—everyone was totally staring when we got here."

He nodded. "You think I didn't notice? I've gotten used to it. Sometimes you just have to do things your way, and realize that not everyone is going to approve. That's sort of my motto. It's helped me survive the past four years—you think it's easy being the weird guy?"

"No, I can't imagine it is. But you seem to be pretty comfortable with who you are."

"Now," Danny agreed. "But when I was a freshman and sophomore, I definitely cared a lot more." He broke off. "Wait a second—what's the name of this guy you're looking for? We have a mission to complete tonight, right?"

"You'll help?" Emily asked. "His name is Ethan."

"Of course I'll help. Now, let's see . . . Ethan . . ." Danny looked around. "You know what? There's one guy named Ethan at Thomas Jefferson—a senior." He started to lead Emily around the room. Weaving through tables of couples, Emily could feel eyes turning to look at her and Danny as they passed. The staring didn't bother her nearly as much as she would have expected. But then again, it wasn't her school, and they weren't her classmates.

Emily really admired Danny's confidence.

A few minutes of meandering—and many, many curious looks—later, Danny stopped suddenly, subtly pointing toward a full table of couples. "There. Is that him?"

Emily squinted. She moved closer so she could see more clearly. The one guy with his back to them . . .

"Is it him?" she whispered to no one in particular. It was possible. Her memory was fuzzy, but the tousled hair, the lean, strong muscles . . . yes, *definitely* possible. She stepped to the side of the table to get a better look at his face, and as she did, the guy leaned in and kissed his date tenderly on the neck. Her stomach sank.

Suddenly the guy turned and looked at her. He was smiling, and a mouth full of braces glinted up at her. Her stomach leaped, realizing that it wasn't Ethan. She was torn between relief (that kiss!) and disappointment (would she ever find him?!). Turning back to Danny, she shook her head.

"No?" he asked, looking as disappointed as Emily felt.

"No," she repeated. "But that's okay. There are other proms." Emily and Danny walked toward Sid and Jeremy, who were still sitting and chatting.

Sid looked up as they approached. "Hey, Em." She smiled. Emily could tell Sid was having a decent time, despite her distaste for prom. "Any luck?" she asked quietly.

"He's not here," Emily replied. "Are you having a good time?"

Sid shrugged. "It's not as bad as it could be." She looked at Jeremy, who was chatting with Danny. "He's nice."

"Yeah," Emily agreed. "So is Danny. I think tonight may not be a total bust," she declared. Suddenly Emily wanted to dance more than anything. She had never danced in skirts and a bustle before.

Fighting against her protestations, Emily dragged Sid off her chair and pulled her toward the dance floor. She beckoned to Danny and Jeremy, and they followed.

Hearing Danny's words echoing through her head, Emily let everyone's stares pass right through her. *After all,* she reasoned, *what fun is dressing in costume if I don't make the most of it?* Caught up in their own semi-Victorian world on the dance floor, the four of them were among the last to leave.

Nine

E: u there?

M: Maybe.

E: can I get a ride 2 charlies?

M: Yeah. How was prom w. Danny?

E: super nice guy, surreal prom.

M: Details?

E: in the car. can we leave soon? my sister is driving me insane.

M: ??

E: she and mom are discussing their "perfect prom night." i do not lie.

M: Nice. I assume this conversation is for your benefit?

E: probably a safe guess. meet u in your front yard in 10?

M: Righty-o.

"Her costume wasn't bad." Sid laughed. She plucked an E string on her guitar, giving it a final twist into tune.

"You honestly wore a corset to prom?" Max had already asked Emily this question three times, and gotten the same answer three times.

Emily nodded her head again, taking a swig of her root beer. "That I did."

Max, Emily, and Charlie were all sitting on amps in the back room of Think, a low-lit club in the Warehouse District downtown. The postprom party for Ridley Prep was about to get under way, and they were helping Sid prepare for her set. As Sid tuned and sound-checked, pretending not to be nervous, Emily entertained the others with the details of their prom the night before. From the preprom portraits to the dance itself, she spared no details.

"And," Emily said, "I'm happy to report that Ethan was *not* at the Thomas Jefferson prom. So the costume didn't really hurt anyone. It was actually a blast."

"A successful prom number four!" Charlie declared. "I can't believe I didn't get to go."

"Trust me, you didn't miss much." Sid was leaning over her guitar, strumming a few chords. She looked up briefly and caught Emily's eye. "Okay, it was pretty fun."

Charlie pointed at her and declared, "You're totally getting into it!"

Sid cracked a smile. "Well, it's better than studying."

"Right?" Emily said, not expecting any kind of answer. "This has definitely been fun. But there are only two more proms to crash after tonight! If Ethan doesn't go to Ridley Prep—which we'll find out tonight—then we have one more weekend of crashing. And the hardest target is up next."

"What's next?" Max asked, swirling his soda around his cup to create a mini liquid tornado. "And are you sure you want to keep doing this? Is this guy really worth it?"

Charlie scoffed. "Are you suggesting we stop now?!" He slapped Max on the head. "Are you crazy? This is just getting good."

"Do you guys want out?" Emily asked. She was totally addicted to the thrill of their mission now, and hadn't realized Max might be having doubts. She was almost happy they hadn't found her crush at one of the first proms, because then they wouldn't have had an excuse to keep crashing. She continued, "Because I can crash the rest of the proms alone." She crossed her arms. "Not that that would be any fun at all." Emily scooted over to her cousin's amp and squeezed in next to him, laying her head on his shoulder. "At least I know I have Charlie to keep me company, right, cuz? It's the boat prom next. . . ."

"You bet!" Charlie declared, wrapping his arm around Emily. "I *love* crashing proms. I can think of no better cure for senior slide than a challenging and dramatic mission. We're like Tom Cruise in *Mission: Impossible*, but before he went all crazy and was still just a slightly too-old action star." Emily hugged him back.

Sid looked up from her guitar. "Are you kidding? I *was* sort of enjoying myself until you compared us to Tom Cruise. Now I'm just offended." She shook her head. "But I have to admit—after last night, I'm totally hooked. I am *so* in for the rest of the proms."

Both Charlie and Emily looked at Max expectantly. He shrugged. "What? It's prom. They're all the same."

"Really?" Emily asked, surprised and

more than a little disappointed. "You're not having fun?"

Max held his hands up in a surrender motion. "I was just saying!" he said, then cracked into his dimpled smile. "But yes, I'm having fun. And definitely still in. Besides, there's a story to be sold after all of this, remember?"

"Good! We're all in!" Emily beamed. "How is your story going, Max? Do you need anything from us?"

Charlie ran his fingers through his hair and offered, "Let me know if you need a physical character description of me for the article. I'd like to make sure you describe me as dapper and striking."

Max shook his head. "That was the plan, Charlie. Just keep your charming personalities and stories coming, and I should be all set. The story's good so far."

"Great," Emily declared, then shifted into planning mode. "So next Friday and Saturday night, we have the last two prom crashes. First up is Northwestern's boat prom on Friday night, followed by East on Saturday. If we can get into Northwestern, we're genius."

"Is it that guarded?" Max asked.

"This is going to be our toughest target," Emily explained, leaning forward. The first prom after-party attendees had begun to stream into the front of Think, and the music had been turned up to compete with the crowd. She raised her voice and continued, "We all know Northwestern is the richest school in the city. We also know that they rent out the Queen Mary yacht every year for their prom. I guess things usually get cooking while they're still docked at the pier on Lake Windham—the whole school piles onboard for their four-course meal, live band, the works. From what I've heard, the school principal personally greets every person boarding the boat. Then the boat takes off—sans principal—and it's just drunken debauchery."

"Debauchery is a great word, Em," Charlie interrupted.

"Thank you." She smiled.

Max interrupted her at this point. "I got a little info from one of the writers at *Buzz*." *Buzz* was the online paper that Max wrote reviews for. "Since almost all of the city's VIPs'—that's very important politicians'—kids go to Northwestern, most of the silliness on the boat is pretty much overlooked by the cops. The bigwigs don't want bad press, so they beg their buddies in the local precincts to turn a blind eye." Max shifted on his amp, getting into his story. "Rumor has it that at least half the school gets puke-up-your-dinner drunk, and things get completely out of control. Most years they have to dock early for fear of someone falling overboard."

"Good info, my man." Charlie nodded appreciatively. "So the question is, how are we going to get on that boat?"

Sid looked up from her guitar. "Someone needs to get a job on the Queen Mary. We need an insider."

They all turned and looked at her. Max slapped his knee. "That's genius!" he said.

"Thank you," Sid responded. "Now, can the three of you all please get the hell out of here? I need to finish getting ready, and you are terrible roadies. I'm much better off on my own."

Charlie stood up. "Touché!"

Emily stood up and passed Sid's pick—which Emily had been rubbing for luck—back to her. "This is it! Are you ready? You sure you don't need anything from us?"

"I'm all good." Sid ran her fingers through

her rumpled hair. "Enjoy the show, all right? And don't tell me if it sucks."

"It will be fantastic!" Emily called over her shoulder as she, Max, and Charlie all slipped out the side stage door and into the main room of the club.

The club was crowded. The room itself was nearly barren, with a small stage carved into one wall. There were two bars running along two other walls of the club, and a few tall tables were set up throughout the room for people to stand around. But the majority of the space in the club had been cleared for dancing, which everyone was already doing.

Most people had changed out of their prom attire into low-slung jeans or more casual dresses. A few male stragglers had left their tuxes on, but loosened their bowties or tied them around their dates' necks. Emily, Max, and Charlie blended into the crowd well. They had packed their prom wear in the car just in case, but the jeans and—in Charlie's case—chinos they were wearing were more than appropriate.

As Emily led the others around the club, searching for Ethan, Charlie cut through the noise to ask, "What does this guy look like again?"

"Hot," she answered seriously. "And yummy."

"That's really helpful," Max said, grabbing a plastic cup with an unidentified dark soda in it off the bar counter. "What color hair does hot and yummy have? And can you not refer to him as 'yummy'? It freaks me out. I picture a pizza or something."

Emily reached out to give Max a little swat in the chest, but he grabbed her arm and pulled her in toward him to prevent the attack. He wrapped her arm behind her back, trapping her in what she was pretty sure she remembered from childhood as a "half nelson." He held her tight against his chest, until she squirmed around to get in his face and fight back.

Their noses were millimeters apart when she turned. Emily's stomach leaped as Max's face settled in close to hers. They'd had this same type of battle a million times since childhood, but she'd never felt anything but a friendly connection, no matter how physically close they got. Until now.

She pulled back, breaking the connection. Max's face cracked into a smile when he said, "What's up, Em? You scared of me? You've never given up *that* easily before."

"No, I just got a little dizzy or something," Emily stammered, shaking her head in confusion. "But you know, it's prom. I'm supposed to act ladylike, not get into brawls with my boorish friends." She pursed her lips and took a dainty swig of her soda.

Charlie, who had been leaning against the bar scanning the crowd for interesting people to talk about, suddenly let out a holler. Sid had just stepped onto the stage and was settling in on a stool. Her guitar was loosely slung around her neck, and her hair was rumpled and messy. She looked like a rock star.

"Yee haw!" Emily yelled, cupping her hands around her mouth as Sid strummed out her first chord. A few Ridley Prep students turned toward at Emily, exchanging looks when they didn't recognize her, Max, or Charlie as one of their own. She smiled at them and raised her hand in a wave, mouthing *hi*. "What?" she asked Max, who was staring at her like she was crazy. "If you act like you fit in, no one notices you. Isn't Charlie and the prom king spectacle the perfect example of that?"

"That's right," Charlie said, staring straight ahead at Sid on stage. "I am the Memorial High Prom King."

After Sid finished her third song and started a mellow ballad, Charlie turned to Emily with a distracted expression on his face. "Remember the other night when you asked me if I had asked Marco to prom?"

"Yeah. Did you bring it up with him?"

"When we were talking last night, I mentioned how much I'm looking forward to prom, and how disappointed I am that he's not going to be here for it. And he just laughed at me."

"Seriously? That doesn't sound like him."

"I think he thought I was joking. But the thing is, I've actually been thinking about it a lot. I don't want to go with Natasha—I'm gay; I want to go with my boyfriend." He paused. "Emily, am I with the wrong guy?"

She turned to look at him. His expression was serious. "You don't really think that, do you?"

"I don't know, Em. I feel like he should know how much prom means to me, and come."

"But unless you tell him, it's not fair to expect that he just *get* that."

Charlie was watching Sid play onstage, but his mind was elsewhere. After a beat, he continued. "I guess I need to figure out how to have the conversation with him. I know it's too late for prom—I'm not ditching Natasha at this point, that would just be mean—but I guess Marco and I have to get a little better at telling each other where things stand." He turned to Emily.

She nodded slowly. "Even I didn't know how much prom meant to you, so I'm not surprised Marco's not getting it."

"*I* didn't know how much prom meant to me until last week." He grinned. "I always thought it was a little bit of a joke. I guarantee this is going to sound lame, but winning prom king at Memorial was seriously one of my highlights of high school. It got me all kicked up about prom."

"Yeah," Emily agreed. "I know what you mean." She smiled and gave Charlie a quick squeeze just as Sid wrapped her last song.

When Sid stood up to leave the stage, everyone cheered and whistled. Her bluesy-rock style had fit in perfectly with the vibe of the Ridley Prep crowd. She stepped off the stage and made her way through the crowd toward her friends at the back of the small club. Her guitar was still strapped around her neck. "So?" she prompted.

Charlie stepped forward first, planting two huge kisses on her forehead. "You!" He held her away from him, studying her face in the club lights. "You were amazing! I mean it. I'm so happy for you."

"You're acting like my grandma after my first communion," Sid said, sneering. "Was it that bad?" She actually looked a little nervous.

"Are you kidding me? I'm so proud to call you my best friend right now. Like I've said three million times before, you're going to be a huge star."

"It was great," Emily seconded. Max nodded and gave Sid a high five.

She looked relieved. "You really thought it was good? Sh—shmack, I was nervous as hell up there."

As they stood recounting all the brilliant moments in Sid's performance, a guy in a Skittles T-shirt and jeans sauntered up to their foursome. He looked familiar, but Emily couldn't place him.

Sid obviously knew the guy, because she

stepped forward and said, "Hey, James."

"Hey," James responded slowly, nodding. "Good set."

Sid's face morphed into a smile. "Thanks." She turned to Emily, Charlie, and Max. "Do you guys know James? He's the lead singer of 1492. James, these are my friends—Emily, Charlie, Max."

"Ohhh," Emily said, nodding. *So that's where I know him from.* 1492 was one of the most popular local bands, and one of Sid's all-time favorites. Their popularity had spread beyond Minnesota's borders, and they were often on tour. But at least half the year they stuck close to home and played a regular Tuesday-night gig at one of the coolest bars in the area, French's.

Sid grinned at James again. "I didn't realize you were . . . shoot! Are you guys playing tonight?" She looked like she could burst, she was so happy.

"Yeah," James said. His voice sounded like molasses: deep, dark, and soulful. "We're headlining, I guess." He smiled slowly, twisting the lower corner of his T-shirt into a spiral. "Do you have a regular gig somewhere?" he asked Sid. "I'd love to come hear you play."

"No, not yet. I'm working on it." She shot Charlie a look that said, *Do not mention the Leaf Lounge.*

"We're looking for someone to open a couple of our shows at French's this month—would you be into that?"

"That'd be amazing." Sid's eyes opened wide, uncomprehending of what had just happened. "Are you messing with me?"

James laughed—it was more of a chortle. "No, I'm not messing with you. Swing by next Tuesday around nine, and we'll get you hooked up. I'll introduce you to the rest of the band and French's owner, Jimmy. I'm sure it'll be cool, but I like to make sure everyone's happy with our opening act. Cool?"

"Cool," Sid said. "See you Tuesday. Thanks, James."

Charlie waited until James was a few feet away before turning to Sid and declaring, "When they produce your *E! True Hollywood Story*, the moment we just witnessed is going to be that part in the show just before a commercial break when the narrator starts getting all excited and says, 'Things were about to change for Sidney Cristina Martinez.' You are going to *open* for 1492!"

"No way," Sid said, shaking her head. "This is *so* not happening."

By the time 1492 hit the stage later that night, Sid had finally begun to believe that what had happened with James was real. She stood sandwiched between Emily, Charlie, and Max, all four of them bouncing gently in time to the music.

As they all sang along to 1492's song "Promises," Emily put her arms around Sid from behind, resting her chin on the top of her friend's head. Charlie and Max each put an arm around the two girls. They hadn't found Ethan, but none of them could deny that this had been the best prom yet.

When Emily got home that night, her mom was waiting up in the family room, reading. Emily poked her head in the door to say good night and make a hasty retreat.

"Come here, honey," her mom said.

Emily stuck one leg into the doorway, hoping that was enough to make her mom feel like she was making an effort. "Why are you still up?"

"I couldn't sleep. When are we going prom dress shopping?" Her mom sat up a little straighter on the couch, pulling her robe closed over her bare legs. "I saw Miriam Arnold at the gym today, and she said Kristi is going with that nice boy you used to see—Dan, isn't it?"

"Yeah, Dan." Emily wasn't sure where this conversation was going, but so far didn't like the tone in her mom's voice. It sounded like comparisons would be coming next, and questions about Emily's love life.

As a teacher at her daughter's high school, Emily's mom was privy to far more information than she should be. For example, she knew Emily had not yet bought her prom tickets, even though they'd been on sale for more than a week. She also knew Emily didn't have a date, but chose to ignore this apparently irrelevant piece of the puzzle.

"Well, she told me that Kristi and her friends are going to the Lighthouse for dinner." Her mom paused, studying Emily in the lamplight. Emily crossed her fingers—it looked like her mom had just gotten distracted. "Where were you tonight? You look sweaty."

Emily swiped her arm across her forehead. "I was out with Charlie, remember? We went to one of Sid's gigs." *Not lying,* she reminded herself. *We were at one of Sid's gigs.*

"It was gross there—hot—I should take a shower. Good night."

She gave her mom a quick kiss, then headed up the stairs to the shower. Emily knew she'd left her mom hanging on the prom conversation. She considered trekking back downstairs to tell her mom about their prom crashing, but once again decided it was a bad idea. Mom would positively die if she knew Emily had been going to proms without giving her a chance to take pictures to commemorate the nights. Not to mention that it was a lot more fun to keep their inappropriate—and bordering on illegal—little escapades to herself. No need to drag the parents into things. There were a lot worse things she could be doing—and wasn't.

There was another reason that she kept climbing the stairs—though Emily barely admitted it to herself. She already felt crappy enough about the fact that she didn't have a date for her own prom. If her mom knew she was on a mission to find the perfect date (a move that, to an outsider, might seem a little desperate), her mom might leap forward and try to fix things for her.

Emily couldn't face the pressure cooker.

As she grabbed her robe and headed toward the bathroom, Emily felt sure she was making the right choice. She needed to deal with this on her own and couldn't manage her mom's expectations on top of her own prom disappointment. She just hoped they would find Ethan the next weekend, or she was going to need to face up to the reality that her prom fantasy wasn't coming true.

Ten

Charlie's head popped out of the top of a stretch white limo. "Let's move!"

Emily waved from her post outside the front entrance of the mall, where she was waiting for her "dates" to pick her up. Her face lit up when she spotted Charlie's head coming around the corner—she hadn't realized he would be picking her up in a limo, but somehow it wasn't all that surprising. "You look happy. What's with the ride?"

"You like? It's my little treat. We deserve to go to one of these proms in style." Charlie tapped his hands on top of the roof of the car. "Hop in."

The limo driver opened the back door for Emily, and she slid onto the leather seat next to Sid, who had her feet resting on the seat across from her. Max saluted her from his spot in the back of the limo. The interior had green and pink lights running through the door paneling. There was a bottle of bubbly submerged in a tub of ice in one of the wall panels. Charlie had a glass poured for himself next to an already-burning clove cigarette perched in the ashtray.

When the driver closed the door behind Emily, Charlie descended from the sunroof and flopped back onto the long seat next to Sid's feet. He squeezed his cigarette between two fingers and took a long drag. Emily grabbed the cigarette from him and stubbed it out. His smoking disgusted her, and Charlie knew it. He didn't smoke that often, but always seemed to light up more around Emily—Charlie liked to push her buttons.

"I am *exhausted*," he declared, lifting his feet onto the seat and leaning back on his elbows.

Emily frowned. "Are you really going to complain? One of us smells like burned coffee right now, and I'm going to guess that's not you since—oh, *that's right*—you got out of work today." Charlie had been scheduled for the Leaf Lounge's after-school shift with Emily but had only been there for about an hour. Emily had agreed it was a good idea for one of them to skip out of work to finalize their plan for that night's prom with Max. Charlie had immediately volunteered to leave. When Gary had come in to take over for the evening shift, Emily had made up some excuse about Charlie getting sick. Then she scooted out of the coffee shop and into the mall's public bathroom to change into her dress before he could ask any questions. "But you're forgiven, on account of this limo."

"Thank you." Charlie exhaled a long, deep breath. "Just so you know, it's not as easy as it might seem to coordinate a four-way prom date. *That's* why I'm so exhausted." He glanced at Sid, whose eyes were closed. "Sid refused to get dressed. Let's just say, I had to take drastic steps to make things happen." Sid kept her eyes closed and smiled in response.

The four of them were on their way to Northwestern's boat prom, where Max would don a waiter's uniform (maroon boat shoes and an all-cotton, machine-washable "tux" with a maroon Queen Mary logo emblazoned on the back) and sneak them into the boat through the service galley. After Sid's brilliant suggestion that one of them get a job on the Queen Mary so they would have an insider working the event, Max had remembered that one of the guys on his dad's curling team was a Queen Mary captain.

It hadn't taken much for Max to convince his dad to help him get a summer job working as a crew member. His parents had been nagging him for months to make some spending money before college in the fall, and the Queen Mary was a perfectly reputable option. Max's dad had pulled through, and Max was now gainfully employed.

As one might have expected, none of the long-standing Queen Mary employees wanted to work the pukefest high school prom with zero tip potential. So that Friday night—the night of Northwestern's boat prom—would be Max's maiden voyage as a busboy. The boat's management had hurried him onto the payroll specifically for this event—Northwestern's prom was *that* bad. Max's first shift started at eight, just in time for the hors d'oeuvres.

Max appraised Emily from the backseat

of the limo and said, "You look nice. Have I seen that dress before?"

"Funny." Emily had worn her prom dress a total of three and a half times—the half was her date with Danny. "You might think the novelty of the dress would have worn off by now, but it hasn't. By the way, Max, the maroon boat shoes? Nice."

"You do look nice in pink, Emily. Your mom always says you should wear it more often." Charlie smirked. He loved to tease Emily about her mom and her nagging ways, particularly since Emily's mom was his aunt, and she treated Charlie like some sort of wonder child. Emily often got the impression she was her parents' third favorite child, behind Abby and Charlie. She really couldn't wait to get out of Minnesota and into her own life in New York.

Emily ignored her cousin's comment and popped her head out the top of the limo. She let her hair blow free in the wind, putting her arms up to catch the air as it circled around her.

When they stopped at a traffic light, Charlie popped out next to her, wearing his Memorial High Prom King crown. The car that was stopped at the light next to them honked. A high-school-age guy in the driver's seat waved—he was wearing a tux. "Seriously?" Emily asked, gesturing to Charlie's crown.

"Why not? It's my badge of honor, and I'm proud to wear it." He turned toward the car that had honked and waved back. "Think that guy's going the same place we are? We already have a friend." Charlie smiled at the driver, who was still waving. "A really, really eager friend."

Emily hoped everyone at Northwestern was as nice and dopey as the guy in the car next to them. They had a big challenge ahead of them, and if they had bitchy students to deal with, it would make their mission that much more complicated. As the limo pulled away from the light, Sid and Max both squeezed out of the sunroof to join them. All four friends lifted their arms and waved at the pedestrians walking past. Emily grinned—though it wasn't her romantic prom fantasy, this version of prom night certainly came close to perfect.

The limo pulled into a circular drive that was packed with other limos and dress- and tux-clad teens. Emily, Sid, Charlie, and Max all slid back into the limo's interior. Sid watched people through the limo's darkened windows, while Charlie adjusted his tie. Checking his watch, Max announced, "Five minutes until my shift. Are we ready?"

Emily twisted her hair into a low knot, which she secured with a few pins. "Come here," Charlie gestured, holding his glass of bubbly loosely in his hand.

"What's wrong?" Emily patted her head nervously. "Is my hair a disaster?"

"Sheesh, chill. It looks great." Charlie pulled a tiny blossom from a small vase in the wall of the limo. He pinned it into Emily's hair, just behind her left ear. "Now it's perfect."

Emily smiled at her cousin. "Thank you. I don't know why I'm so nervous. I guess since there are only two proms left, the chance of finding Ethan tonight is that much higher." She adjusted her dress, fiddling with a wrinkle that had formed over her thigh.

"That's why we need to get in there." Charlie poked his head out the roof of the limo, then popped back down again. "You ready, Em?"

"We're on." Emily's stomach made a nervous little flip. "Let's move."

The driver opened the door of the limo for

them. Max jumped out, followed by a surly-looking Sid. Charlie quickly directed the driver to wait until they returned to the dock later that night. Then he held his hand out for his cousin. "Take my arm," he instructed.

Emily did as she was told, and they followed Max and Sid toward the dock. The other prom attendees were boarding the enormous tour yacht via a ramp that led onto the fore deck. There were tables piled high with appetizers and mocktails, none of which had yet been touched. Most of the prom crowd was still mingling on the dock, comparing outfits and preparty stories.

Max stopped at a small gift shop that sold souvenirs and tickets for the Queen Mary and other dinner boats. The gift shop was also the office and home base for the boats' employees—Max stepped inside the shop to punch in for his shift. When he returned to the dock, he handed Sid, Emily, and Charlie each a white chef's smock to put on over their formal wear. "Everyone ready to work?" Max winked.

The other three followed Max past the prom revelers and moved farther down the dock toward the aft deck. Max greeted a few of the Queen Mary waiters who were standing near a second ramp that was being used to load catering gear into the boat's galley. Other tux-clad employees bustled past the foursome, who had stopped a few feet short of the ramp.

Max glanced at the other employees, all of whom were too uninterested and/or busy to notice the newcomers. No one seemed to care that Charlie, Emily, and Sid were wearing formal wear under their smocks—as long as they were helping, it seemed they were invisible.

On Max's cue, Emily grabbed a steaming platter of dumplings off a rolling cart on the dock. Charlie followed suit, turning up his nose at his permanently stained uniform and groaning under the weight of the hot plate he was carrying. Sid lifted a small crate of freshly washed plates off the dock.

They stepped one at a time onto the long, wobbly ramp and paraded into the boat's galley. Inside the galley, Emily set down her dumplings and pulled off her uniform to reveal her dress again. She straightened the perma-wrinkle over her thigh, slid out the galley door, up a few short stairs, and onto the expansive yacht's deck. Charlie and Sid were steps behind her. Max waved to them from down in the galley, then returned to work.

Their plan had worked. They were in.

Moving to the front of the boat, Emily, Charlie, and Sid slipped into the crowd easily. There were several groups of people gathered near the buffet table, and many more parading onto the boat. Charlie scanned the crowd. "I don't see anyone who fits your description of Mr. Yummy."

"Me either." Emily twisted her hair nervously. "But I do see a lot of flasks out and in use. Max was right about this prom—there will be a lot of drunk people on this boat tonight."

Sid nodded to a guy on the other side of the deck. "That guy's already down for the count." Emily looked in the direction Sid had gestured. There was a tall, out-of-shape guy sitting on one of the benches, resting his forehead on his knees.

"It's only eight!" Emily giggled. "Looks like he's not gettin' lucky tonight." The drunk guy's date was standing at his side, one hand clutched around her cell phone, the other patting one of his shoulders. She looked pissed and embarrassed.

The three friends chatted and strolled around the main deck while the rest of Northwestern's students piled on board. Soon the boat pulled away from the dock and set sail into the inky black night. The Queen Mary was crowded and loud, and Emily was starting to feel a little seasick and smushed. She wanted to escape but was stuck in the middle of Lake Windham.

While appetizers were passed, Emily weaved her way through the main deck alone but didn't see Ethan anywhere. Many people had moved into the well-lit and festive covered area on the main deck, where dinner was being served. A few lone couples stood on the outer deck, giggling and kissing in the moonlight. Charlie and Sid had followed a few of Charlie's new friends into the dining room, where Emily could see them laughing through the windows.

The appetizers had been cleared from the front deck and the tables had been folded up for storage. The front of the boat was now decorated with tiny, glowing lights that blew gently in the breeze.

Emily breathed in the clean, cool night air. She held on to the railing circling the deck and strolled back toward the rear of the boat. A circular staircase led her upward to a smaller, unpopulated deck overlooking the main level of the boat.

"Hey, you." Max's voice cut through the stillness of the night, surprising Emily.

She turned, seeing her best friend perched on an overturned plastic crate in one corner of the back deck, looking out over the lake. He was surrounded by dirty appetizer dishes piled high with food. "Hey," she replied.

"No Ethan, huh?"

"Seems that way." She moved toward Max's dish outpost, leaning back on a railing. "Charlie and Sid are having a good time."

"You're not?"

"Not really," she said, blowing her long bangs out of her eyes. "Can I help?" Emily offered.

Max held a dirty plate out to her. "Scrape, then stack." Emily nodded and pushed the food off one of the dirty plates into a big garbage bin propped up next to the railing. "You don't need to help though."

"I know." She grabbed another plate, carefully keeping it away from her borrowed dress. "This is really disgusting."

"No kidding. You'll notice I'm on my own out here." Max grimaced and scraped. "New guy."

"The job suits you," Emily teased.

"This is making me appreciate the college career ahead of me. I don't think I'm cut out for dish duty the rest of my life." He paused and looked up at Emily. "But I'm going to miss this."

Emily turned to him. Her stomach knotted like it had at the Ridley Prep post-prom the weekend before. "Me too." She set her now-empty plate in the plastic dishwasher tray Max was stacking plates in. "These last few weeks have been really fun. I'm going to miss you guys. You especially . . . and Wisconsin is really far from New York."

"Nine hundred eighty-four miles to Appleton from Manhattan." Max cocked his head to the side and smirked. "MapQuest. I'm preparing for my Emily withdrawal. I thought you were dying to get out of here. Haven't you been counting the days?"

"Yeah," Emily admitted. "But I sort of forget that when I leave *here*, I'm also leaving you and Charlie and Sid. And painful as it is to admit it, I think I'm going to miss my little sister a tiny bit."

"Don't worry about that," Max said seriously. "I bought you a clock that has her voice recorded on it. Every hour, on the hour, Abby will announce: 'It's one o'clock! Do you miss me, Emily? It's two o'clock, do you want a snack, Emily?'"

Emily laughed. "I assume you're kidding, but I wouldn't put something like that past you. Man, Max, I'm gonna be a mess without you next year. Who's going to keep me up to date on the news of the weird?"

"I think you'll find plenty of bizarre stuff in Manhattan. I'm going to seem normal comparatively. Besides, Charlie is what, like an hour away?"

"Is Yale that close to New York?" Emily shuddered. "I didn't really think about that. That's a little too close for comfort."

Max laughed. "You'd probably be lonely way out there by yourself. But if anyone can handle New York, it's you."

"Yeah," Emily agreed. "I'll be all right."

"Oh, hey," Max interrupted, grinning in the moonlight. "I sold my prom crashers story!"

Emily grinned back. "Really? Max, that's fantastic. To *Buzz*?"

"Yep. It's going online Sunday. I'm in

edits now. I have to write up the rest of the proms before I turn in my final draft. They definitely want me to use the stuff from tonight and tomorrow night—our last prom—before I finish up. But you're going to be famous. As 'Emmy,' though, not Emily. They made me change names."

"I would hope. I can't believe you didn't tell me about this. It really is going to be hard next year. I see you every day now, and still I feel like I'm missing things."

Max laughed. "I just found out yesterday."

"So? This is just a sneak peek of what next year's going to be like. Do you promise to IM with me every day?"

"Maybe," he teased. When Emily threatened to drop a plate of discarded food in his lap, he laughed. "Yeah, yeah, I promise!"

"Good." Emily set down her plate and leaned against the railing, looking out into the dark lake. After a few minutes of silence she murmured, "It's really pretty here. I sometimes forget."

Max nodded. "It's not bad." He scraped silently, studying Emily in the dim spotlight illuminating the back deck of the boat. After a few moments, he asked quietly, "Why aren't you having fun tonight?"

She turned, sighing. "This whole prom thing is starting to really get to me." She tucked a stray piece of hair behind her ear when the wind blew it loose. "I know it's just a dance, but I guess I always thought prom would really be *something* for me, you know? Romance and flowers and, well, the whole thing. . . . I thought I had maybe found that when I met Ethan a few weeks ago. But now things are starting to feel a little . . ." She broke off.

"Hopeless?" Max offered, not-so-helpfully.

"Yeah." Emily winced. "Thanks."

"I don't think it's hopeless. And I don't think it's unreasonable that you're looking for all that. You wouldn't be Emily if you just went to prom the way everyone else goes to prom. This prom crashing thing—that's how the Emily Bronson *I* know and love would want to do prom. It makes it an adventure. It seems to me that you *have* gotten your prom thing out of your system. Would you give up all this"—he gestured around at the boat—"for just a regular, ordinary prom? Would a good date with pretty white teeth really fulfill your every fantasy?" Max was gesturing wildly by the end of his little speech, and inadvertently

flung a fork off the edge of the boat. "Oops."

Emily laughed and leaned forward to give Max a hug. He reached up from his seat on the crate, his arms stretching around her waist. The hug was clumsy, but warm and comfortable. Max's arms wrapped around Emily's waist and he pulled her in close. When he did, she felt the same suspicious spark in her chest and pulled back—this was getting ridiculous. She shivered in the cool breeze, rubbing her arms to keep them warm.

Max stood up from his crate and moved closer to Emily. "Are you cold?" he asked, concerned.

"I'm fine." But she wasn't fine. She wasn't sure if it was the slow prom song playing in the background or the lake setting (though scraping food remains wasn't particularly romantic) or her companion himself, but Emily was once again feeling an awkward electricity around Max.

"You're not fine," Max said. "You're cold. Come here." He moved forward, bundling her in his arms. Emily relaxed into his shoulder, only slightly aware of Max's dirty uniform. She tucked her arms in against his chest and her ear brushed his.

Her whole body was tensed up with the

delicious feeling of what might happen. She leaned back and met Max's eyes in the moonlight, and they both smiled. Emily was surprised to discover how natural—and yet totally new—their connection felt. Max pulled her back in toward him, tipping his face toward hers.

Just then Emily heard Charlie's yell from the lower deck. She pulled out of Max's arms and leaned over the railing to look for her cousin. Charlie spotted her and yelled again. "Em! We have to go. Now!"

"Now?" Emily asked, a smile tugging the corners of her lips. "We're on a boat, Charlie." Max leaned over the railing next to her and waved at Charlie and Sid.

"Hey, Max," Charlie said, grinning mischievously.

A loud, booming grunt came from the front deck of the boat, then a guy yelled, "Where is that dude? I'm gonna kill him!"

"Trust him," Sid announced in a loud whisper. "We need to get out of here. Em, are you in or out?"

Without thinking, Max quickly unhinged one of the lifeboats hanging next to him and lowered it to the water. "Go," he told Emily. "Take the spiral staircase down. There's a ladder just there." He pointed over the rail at a white wooden ladder hanging from the lower deck into the water. "There are oars in the boat. I'll explain to the captain somehow—luckily it's one of the college guys driving the boat tonight, so he should be cool about it."

Emily was confused. So confused. What had just almost happened? She didn't think she was imagining it—but had she and Max maybe just almost kissed? It was so unexpected and strange and thrilling, all at once.

Charlie was gesturing wildly from the lower deck and had begun to climb down the ladder and into the lifeboat bobbing gently in the water below. Sid was already in. Emily could see lights from the lakeshore just a few hundred yards away. She knew if they got into the lifeboat, they would be on dry land in just a few minutes if they rowed hard—though the rowing would, of course, be up to her and Sid. Surely Charlie's little getaway plan didn't allow for any exertion on his part.

The spiral staircase was wet, and Emily felt her shoes slip. She pulled them off and crossed the deck to the ladder. In less than thirty seconds, all three were safely aboard the lifeboat and Max had untied the ropes from the Queen Mary. They were free.

Laughing maniacally, Charlie leaned back into the bench in the lifeboat. Emily pulled the oars out and dipped them in the water. Sid was hunched over laughing in the front of the boat. "*What* did you do?"

Charlie was too hysterical to talk and just pointed. An almost naked guy was standing on the front deck of the boat, staring after them, waving his fist in the air and swearing.

Emily's eyes widened. But it wasn't because of Charlie or the naked guy or the fact that they were stuck in a lifeboat in the middle of Lake Windham.

She was staring at the deck of the boat, where a crowd of Northwestern students had gathered to watch their lifeboat drift away and chuckle at their naked classmate. There, in the middle of the crowd, yummy as a slice of Max's mom's cake, stood Ethan, just as gorgeous as Emily remembered him.

"Emily?" Ethan had seen her, too. He was shouting over the noise of the crowd to be heard.

Emily nodded. Lifting an oar, she shouted, "Hi, Ethan," as waves carried the lifeboat away and the yacht blurred into twinkling lights in the distance.

Eleven

Emily yawned and slurped a mouthful of milky coffee. It had been twelve hours since they'd left Northwestern's prom on a lifeboat, and she'd slept four of them. Now she was slumped behind the counter at the Leaf Lounge, downing coffee and waiting for the first morning regulars to arrive.

She, Charlie, and Sid had gotten to shore quickly the night before. They had tied the lifeboat to a post on the dock and climbed into their waiting limo. Emily still couldn't understand the full story of what had happened that made them have to abandon ship so quickly—Charlie started gagging on his laughter every time he tried to tell the story, and Sid just kept shaking her head and saying Charlie needed to tell it.

But Charlie had spluttered out enough for Emily to know that the big naked guy had, for some unidentifiable reason, removed his tux to puke up his preprom drinks in the ship's toilet, at which point Charlie had apparently led a little gang of other drunk people to grab the guy's clothes from outside the bathroom door as a fun prank.

Charlie had stowed them in one of the ship's life jacket containers, and the guy had emerged from the bathroom in boxers, socks, and a raging prehangover. He had sobered up slightly during his pukefest, and was embarrassed and angry about his missing clothes. Charlie's laughter hadn't helped to calm him down.

Apparently a bunch of the guy's friends had threatened to throw Charlie overboard as payback, which is when he had yelled to Emily, interrupting her and Max's almost moment.

She felt her thoughts once again drifting back to the strangely electric hug from the night before. She pushed them to the side of her mind, recognizing that years of friendship don't change overnight. She would never risk losing Max as a friend to pursue any feelings that might be there. Things would be so awkward between them if she were wrong and she said something to Max—he would think she'd gone crazy.

And anyway, she had now (sort of) found Ethan. There was still a little glimmer of hope that she would get to go to her own prom as one half of a developing couple. He went to Northwestern. Now she just needed to track him down on Facebook or MySpace or something.

The key was making that seek-and-find seem as unstalkeresque as possible. He obviously remembered her—but had he been interested enough during their first meeting to think it was normal that she had gone to so much effort to track him down? It was doubtful that he would appreciate the humor of prom crashing as much as Max, Charlie, and Sid. In fact there was a pretty good chance he'd think she was sort of psycho.

Emily was staring off into space, resting her lips on the rim of her coffee cup. She hadn't noticed anyone come into the shop, so she started a bit when a deep male voice roused her from her daydreaming. "Hi."

She looked up, pushing her bangs from her eyes. "Hi," she repeated quietly. Ethan stood on the other side of the counter. He was hotter and tastier-looking than ever. And he had come to find her! "How are you?"

"I'm okay." A smile played at the edge of Ethan's mouth. He had something to say to her, but was measuring his words carefully.

Emily smiled. "Another chai?" she asked. She really hoped he wasn't there for chai. *Oh,* she thought suddenly. *What if he is?*

"I guess I got the hint," Ethan said suddenly and awkwardly. He was smiling, but looked a little uncomfortable. "I'm still waiting for that call you promised."

Emily stared back at him. He was waiting for her call! "It's a long story," she said. "But let's just say that I definitely *did not* mean to give you the impression that I did. I *definitely* wanted to call you." She paused. "Give me your cell," she blurted out suddenly. Ethan obliged, and Emily punched her number into his phone. "Now you have my number, and it's on you to call me."

"Well, maybe I don't want to call you," Ethan said. Emily frowned—had she totally misread the signals? Ethan continued, "Maybe I'd rather just make plans right now. Honestly, I don't really trust you to follow up." He grinned mischievously. "What time are you off work?"

Nice, she thought. *A take-charge guy.* "Three."

"Can I come by and pick you up?"

Emily's stomach fluttered. "Sure."

"Good." Ethan grinned. "See you then." When he got to the door, he turned back. "Do I seem like a stalker for coming here to ask you out?" he asked.

Emily laughed. "Just a little bit." She raised her hand and held her thumb and forefinger close together. "Honestly, though, I can think of a lot crazier things you could have done."

But we'll save that conversation for another time, she mused, smiling at the memory of the past few weeks. *I just hope he can appreciate a good story.*

"I hope you like this place." Ethan pushed aside a branch, guiding Emily along a rocky path.

Emily tilted her chin up, inhaling the scent of the pine needle canopy above her. "How far are we going?" she asked. She studied Ethan's calf muscles as they propelled him forward on the path in front of her. She was enjoying the view and wasn't eager to stop walking yet.

"Just a little bit farther. Are you hungry?"

Ethan turned to look at Emily, concerned.

"I will be. But I can wait." She smiled. "Thanks for asking."

Ethan grinned back at her again, the corners of his mouth crinkling. "Good. I have a ton of food. I don't want to eat alone, so you better be hungry." Emily took this as a good sign, since she had never been one of those girls that didn't like to eat. She *loved* food. Ethan had a backpack slung casually over one shoulder that was stuffed with tasty treats. Emily could see a dark chocolate bar peeking out of the slightly open compartment. Her mouth watered.

They had been making small talk since Ethan had picked her up from the Leaf Lounge a half hour earlier. They chatted about the usual subjects—school, family—and she couldn't believe it when he told her he would be going to Columbia University in New York City that fall. They would be only a hundred blocks apart. While they talked, Ethan drove to a little hiking trail that crawled along a brook just a few miles from the mall. It was a gorgeous trail—she couldn't believe she hadn't known it was there.

Emily had no idea how exhilarating a date could be. Strange and awkward sorta-dates she knew all about. The few losers she'd "dated" had been friends of friends before she had made the mistake of taking things to the next level. She'd never actually been out—on a bona fide date!—with a guy she was really into.

Except Ethan. So she really didn't want to mess this up.

"I hope you don't mind me asking you this. . . . Why were you on a lifeboat on Lake Windham last night? Were you at my prom?" Ethan kept walking, staring straight forward. "Do I want to know?"

"Well," Emily started, smirking to herself, "that's an interesting story."

Ethan suddenly stopped at a grove of trees that formed a sort of canopy over a clearing on the ground. The grass was soft and fluffy, and the river gurgled and splashed nearby. "We're here," he said, pulling the backpack off his shoulder and tossing it on the ground.

"It's gorgeous," Emily murmured.

"So what's the story?"

"What?" Emily asked, settling into a cross-legged position on the ground in the middle of the grassy knoll. "Oh! The prom thing." She smiled self-consciously as Ethan looked at her from his seat on the grass. Then she reluctantly started from the beginning and told him everything.

She realized it was better to go for full disclosure and let him make his decision about her based on the truth. So she told him about how his number had been smudged away, told the stories about Neil and Danny and the crazy costume, and finally about Max getting a job on the Queen Mary so they would have an in at Northwestern. As she talked, she noticed Ethan's eyes widening in disbelief. When she got to the end of the story—Lake Windham—he whistled. "So you were just looking for me?" He cocked an eyebrow.

"No!" Emily covered her eyes with her hands. "Well, initially, yes. But ultimately, my friends and I were just sort of looking for something fun to do. Proms were a good challenge. And who doesn't love going to prom?"

"Gotcha. So I was secondary to the bigger mission?" Ethan grinned. "An innocent bystander?"

Emily groaned through a smile. "This is all coming out wrong." She lay her chin on her knees, which were bent up toward her face.

"I'm teasing you," Ethan said, grabbing one of Emily's knees. She looked up when he touched her. "I think it sounds like a lot of fun. It's flattering that I inspired something so cool."

His hand lingered on her knee a few seconds longer than it needed to, and Emily shivered despite the warm day.

Intentional? she wondered. *Flirting?* She could only hope.

"So you don't think we're crazy?" she asked, hiding part of her face behind her knees. "I guess I would if I were in your shoes. You have to know my friends to get them."

"They sound cool," he said, pulling the chocolate bar out of his backpack. "I hope I get to meet them." He broke open the chocolate bar wrapper and offered her a piece. "I have some sandwiches and stuff, too. But I'd rather start with dessert. You mind?"

Emily shook her head happily. "Nope." She grabbed the chocolate. "So now that I've told you about prom crashing, it's your turn. What's something crazy you've done?"

"Honestly . . ." Ethan chewed his chocolate as he spoke. "Not much. I've been pretty focused on soccer and getting good grades, so I haven't really done anything too wild. We toilet-papered a guy's house once for soccer, but we got caught. So that was maybe crazy, but not so fun."

"That doesn't count. Come on," Emily pushed. "There must be something."

Ethan suddenly stood up. "I just thought of something. Follow me." He left his backpack sitting on the patch of grass and led Emily a few yards farther down the trail. Moments later they came to an old wooden bridge that carried the wooded path up and over a deep, wide portion of the river. "I've been swimming here a hundred times."

"It's tempting," Emily interrupted. *What does he have in mind?*

"But I've never jumped." Ethan smiled at Emily, pulling off his shirt. His broad chest was a golden brown—obviously a regular "skins" player on his soccer team—and lean and muscular. He was wearing only green athletic shorts, and Emily was definitely impressed. "My buddies and I come here a lot, and everyone else always jumps off the bridge into the water. I always avoid it and climb in from the shore down below. What do you say?"

Emily leaned over the edge of the bridge. The water was at least twenty feet below them. Her heart began to race, a little out of fear, a little out of anticipation. "I'm in," she said, smiling broadly. "Are you sure?"

"I'm not gonna lie—I'm afraid of heights." Ethan rubbed his arms. "But I'm pumped." He clapped his hands and whooped, making Emily laugh. Ethan was goofy—in a good way.

"You're doing this for me?" she asked, lifting an eyebrow.

"Hey, you crashed proms for me. That has to take courage. I need to even things up, right?"

Emily nodded. "I'll go if you will." She was glad she was wearing her cute, red boy shorts under her jeans that day. They were just as covering as a bathing suit and a little sexy-cute to boot. She thanked her lucky stars that she'd worn the black tank top instead of her white one to work—wet and white would have left very little to the imagination.

She peeled off her jeans and hoped Ethan's fear had paralyzed his eyesight. She wasn't sure she was prepared for the full-body once-over. He politely averted his eyes.

Together they moved toward the edge of the bridge, and each of them sat on the wooden platform. "On the count of three?" Ethan suggested.

"One," Emily started. They dangled their legs off the edge of the bridge.

"Two," Ethan grabbed her hand.

"Three!" they shouted together. Then they both scooted forward and off the edge of the bridge. Emily could feel Ethan's hand tighten around hers as they fell forward. The force of the water broke their hands apart, but Ethan sought hers again as their bodies popped through the surface of the water. When they emerged from the murky river, they were both laughing and sputtering water. Emily adjusted her tank top to make sure nothing had fallen out.

"That was great!" Emily exclaimed, pulling herself up onto a big rock on shore that was warm from the sun. "You really haven't done that before?"

Ethan grinned. "Okay, maybe that's not quite true." His eyes were alive with laughter. "But I wanted to make sure you'd go in with me." Emily swatted him playfully as he climbed onto the rock next to her.

"You *have* jumped before?"

He nodded. "But it's never been that fun."

"You totally had me going. I thought I was helping you overcome this great, momentous fear." Emily shook her head. "I feel so used."

"I can't apologize. It was worth it. You looked so cute scooting off the edge of the bridge." Emily reddened at the compliment. "Am I in trouble?"

"Yes," she declared. "Now you owe me." She was flirting and knew it was working.

Ethan maneuvered on the rock so he was right next to Emily, almost touching her legs with his. His hand was at his side, and his fingers lightly touched her thigh as he shifted position. Emily watched them and moved her own hand to her side to meet his fingers. Her heart was racing.

"Does this make up for it?" Ethan asked, then turned her face toward his and lifted her chin so her lips touched his. His mouth was wet from the river, and his eyelashes were beaded with water. Emily closed her eyes, soaking in the heat of the sun, the warmth of the rock beneath her, and the strength of Ethan's hand clutching hers. The kiss was short, timid.

"Mmmm," Emily murmured as she pulled back just slightly. "That makes up for it." She smiled, relaxing into a second kiss. Ethan adjusted on the rock so he was facing Emily. She sat cross-legged, leaning in toward him. His legs were spread into a crooked *V*, wrapped around her in a leg hug.

They sat like that for a long time, kissing and laughing and teasing each other. They chatted easily about a million things—their friends, families, college—and only separated for a few minutes when Ethan ran up the hill to grab their clothes and bring food back to the rock.

When the sky began to get dark and a chill crept into the air, they were still talking. Ethan pulled a blanket out of his backpack and spread half of it on the rock beneath them. He snuggled her in so that her back rested against his chest, his legs still wrapped around her. Ethan pulled the rest of the blanket in close to their bodies, tucking them in under the stars.

She felt protected, refreshed, and exhilarated. Ethan was amazing, and she couldn't think of a better first date. She lay her head back, resting it on his shoulder and staring up at the sky.

"Can I ask you something?" she whispered, tilting her neck so she could see his face.

"Mmm-hmm," he murmured back.

"This might sound silly, but . . ." Emily paused. She was suddenly a little nervous. "Would you go to my prom with me?"

Ethan laughed, squeezing his arms around her stomach. "Were you scared to ask me that?" She nodded vigorously, laughing with him. "Of course I will."

"Really? It's next weekend." Emily turned her body so she was facing him.

"Yeah, definitely. It will be fun."

"Fab." Emily beamed. Ethan hugged her close and she smiled contentedly. Suddenly she felt a niggling of paranoia. "Oh, no," she said, sitting up suddenly. "What time is it?"

He pulled his watch out of the backpack. "Eight fifteen." Ethan pulled her back toward him. "Does it matter?"

"Yes!" Emily cried out, sounding more panicked than she would have liked. "I'm supposed to be at our last prom at eight. I promised Max I'd be there. He needs this for his story."

Ethan looked confused. "Story?"

"I'll explain it in the car. Can you drive me to the Maritime Hotel?" She stood up, hastily stuffing the remnants of their picnic into Ethan's backpack. She pulled her cell phone out of her pocket. No service. "He's going to be pissed." She knew it was crappy and self-centered of her to stand up her friends because she was on a date. They would probably understand, but she wanted to help Max see his story through to the end and worried she may have messed things up by being late.

Ethan folded the blanket and stuffed it in his backpack. "Okay," he said, tossing the pack over his shoulder. "Let's go." He grinned at her in the moonlight. "I've had a great time, Emily." He pushed her bangs away from her face and kissed her forehead. "Thanks for finding me."

"Me too," she responded truthfully. Then she climbed back up the steep bank to the main path and out toward Ethan's car.

Twelve

Half an hour later, Ethan pulled his car into the circular driveway of the Maritime Hotel. Max was standing outside the hotel's revolving door, tuxedoed and alone. Emily could tell from the look on his face that he was irritated.

Emily stepped out of the car in her jeans and tank top and approached him. "Hey," she said, heart pounding. She hadn't prepared herself for seeing him again after their almost moment the night before. She felt awkward with him, especially knowing Ethan was in his car behind her. "I'm really sorry I'm late."

"You know what?" Max said, barely looking at her. "It's no big deal. We already went in—just snuck in a side door and checked things out. I got what I needed for the story."

"You went in without me?"

"We waited for an hour—it was pretty obvious you weren't coming."

"Max, I'm sorry." As she said it, she noticed Charlie's car pulling up to the front of the hotel from the parking lot.

"Seriously," Max said blandly, "don't worry about it. I figured I'd wait a few more minutes, just in case you showed up. Charlie and Sid went to get the car. Is that the guy? He was on the boat last night?"

Emily turned to look at Ethan, who was watching them from the driver's seat of his car. "Yeah, that's Ethan."

"Hey," Max called to Ethan, waving halfheartedly at him. Ethan waved back.

Charlie pulled his car up to the front of the hotel, then poked his head out the window to chide, "Well, well, lookie who decided to show up."

Emily flushed. "I'm sorry," she said again. "I didn't realize I was this late."

"Well," Charlie said, "you are. And now Sid and I are late for our prom. In case you've forgotten that one as well, South's prom is tonight. Luckily, Natasha's driving with a group of girls, so we're meeting there. So your lateness didn't totally screw up her night as well."

Emily groaned. She had almost derailed Max's article, and now she'd made Charlie late for his own prom. "Can I make it up to you?" she offered.

Charlie grinned. "That's the spirit!" he said. "Come with us to South's prom. Crash it."

"You're on," Emily agreed. She leaned into the window to address Sid. "Sid, are you going to your prom? When did that happen?"

"I'm playing!" she declared.

Charlie clarified. "Now that she's the opening band for 1492, Marisa Sanchez and the prom committee are all into Sid. They called her this morning *begging* her to play a set."

"Then I'm definitely in. Any chance to hear my favorite singer-songwriter play. Okay if I bring Ethan?"

"Yeah." Charlie shrugged. "Max, you're in, right?" Max was standing behind Emily on the sidewalk. He was quiet. *Maybe,* Emily thought, *it's my imagination, but something seems off.*

"No, I don't think so," he responded. "I have to finish writing my story."

"You have to come," Emily declared. Though she wasn't sure if that was really what she felt. She didn't know if she was prepared to be with him and Ethan at the same time.

Charlie whined, "Yeah, Max, come on. It's the perfect ending to your article."

"Um, okay," he agreed blandly. He opened the back door to Charlie's Volvo and stepped in. "I'll go. I don't have much choice, since you were supposed to give me a ride home."

Emily was now standing alone on the sidewalk, uncomfortable when she realized she wouldn't be riding with her friends, as usual. Emily's dress was in Charlie's car—she had been leaving it in there after most of the proms so that her mom wouldn't get suspicious—and she pulled it out of the trunk now, holding the shimmery fabric in her arms. Charlie gestured to Ethan. "See if he has anything to wear. Then you guys can follow us there."

She nodded and returned to Ethan's car. He rolled down the window and she leaned in. "Hey," she breathed. "Do you have any interest in coming to my cousin's prom with us?" Emily sort of expected him to say no. So far, he was a little too good to be true.

"Absolutely," he answered quickly. "And this is your lucky day," he continued. "My tux is in the trunk." In a move that could only be classified as lucky, Ethan had put his tux in his car that morning, intending to return it to the rental place that afternoon. But his date with Emily had run over and he hadn't had a chance.

"Great," she said. "Then we're good to go."

Twenty minutes later, Emily and Ethan pulled up at South's prom. Charlie, Sid, and Max had already gone into the ballroom. Emily and Ethan had stopped along the way so that they could change into their formal wear in a gas station restroom. As they approached the door to the dance, Ethan turned to Emily and declared, "This is exciting," then leaned over to give her a kiss. Her lips burned.

Inside, they had no trouble getting into prom. No one was guarding the doors, and people were coming and going freely.

Ethan looked a little disappointed.

Emily quickly spotted Max, who was standing by himself against one wall of the ballroom. She led Ethan toward her best friend, realizing again how uncomfortable she felt about having her two guys alone together. Had Max felt their connection the night before too? Was he feeling as uncomfortable around Emily as she was with him?

Once introductions were out of the way, the three of them stood silently for a few minutes, taking in everything around them. Emily was acutely aware of her position, standing between her hot new crush, Ethan, and best-friend-with-potential-spark, Max. Ethan had his hand resting lightly in the curve of her back.

After a few minutes of desperate searching, Emily finally noticed Charlie and his date, Natasha, across the room. She waved madly to get his attention. He left Natasha with her friends and came sashaying over. "This must be the yummy guy you've been talking about," Charlie declared, ignoring Emily and giving Ethan the once-over.

Ethan reached his hand out toward Charlie. "Ethan." He pretended he hadn't heard Charlie's comment. "You must be Charlie."

"When does Sid go on?" Emily asked Charlie.

"Yo!" Sid broke through the noise of the prom by shouting at them from across the room.

Ethan turned to Emily. "Sidney?" he guessed. She nodded.

"I am flipping nervous," Sid declared, storming over to them. She looked at Ethan suspiciously.

Emily smiled at Sid. "Nerves really do bring out the best in you, Sid. This is Ethan, prom guy."

"Oh, right." Sid sized him up. "Good to finally meet you. Hey, what happened after we left your prom last night?"

Emily clutched Ethan's hand at her side. She caught Max sneaking a peek as their fingers intertwined. He averted his gaze.

Ethan laughed. "Brian finally found his tux, but ended up puking on it later. So he probably would have been better off without it. You sort of did the guy a favor by taking it in the first place. He stunk at the after-prom party."

"Once again," Charlie declared proudly,

"a successful prom crash on all accounts." He broke off, pointing to the stage area, where a DJ was playing eighties classics. One of Charlie's drama club cronies—the guy responsible for lighting—was beckoning Sid to the stage.

"I guess this is it . . . ," she said. She clapped her hands twice. "No amount of adrenaline can get you through the nerves of playing in front of your whole school. This is just messed up," she said, then turned to Charlie. "Enjoy the rest of your night, Charles." She winked cryptically, then strode off toward the stage.

"What did that mean?" Emily asked Charlie.

Charlie stared after her. "No clue." He waved at Natasha, who was dancing with a bunch of their friends. Natasha had tied the hem of her ankle-length black slip dress into a knot near her knees to free her legs for dancing. She looked bohemian and chic, twirling and spinning in time to the music.

"Are you and Natasha having a good time?" Emily asked. When she did, Ethan released her hand and put his palm in the small of her back again. Her skin tingled where his hand connected with her body, then the tingle expanded outward like a firecracker. She turned to smile at him, eager to be alone again.

Charlie nodded. "Yeah, I'm having fun. I don't necessarily think she cares that we're here together—she just wanted to go to prom. Which is good, I suppose, since I'm hanging out with you guys." He grinned.

Suddenly a static-filled shout broke through the room. Members of the prom committee were standing onstage, and one of the girls had shouted into the microphone to get everyone's attention. People covered their ears and turned toward the stage. "Sorry," she said with a shrug. "Okay, everybody, we have an amazing surprise for you all tonight. First, we're going to announce this year's prom king and queen, and then"—she paused, relishing in the suspense—"our very own Sidney Marquez—" Emily winced . . . that wasn't even Sid's last name. Ouch. One of the other girls onstage whispered something to the girl with the mic. Mic girl continued, "Sorry, Sidney Martinez, is going to play a few songs to finish our year in style! Our very own South High music celebrity!"

Everyone clapped, and Charlie laughed.

He leaned over to Emily, Ethan, and Max. "It's funny to see Sid at such a school-spirit-heavy event. This is just so out of character for her." Emily laughed and nodded, but Max just stood silently, staring forward. "She must be dying backstage." Charlie chuckled.

"So first"—mic girl waved an envelope over her head—"on behalf of the junior year prom committee, I'm delighted to announce this year's prom king and queen!" The DJ turned on a CD with cheesy drum-roll music. "This year's prom queen is . . . oh, this comes as no surprise to anyone . . . Marisa Sanchez!"

A pretty brunette in the middle of the room feigned surprise and waved her hands in front of her face. The whole room was cheering and clapping, and Marisa managed to muster up a few tears of happiness. She made her way toward the stage to collect her crown.

"And now," mic girl announced, "we'll reveal Marisa's king! Drumroll please. . . . This year's South High Prom King is . . . Charlie Delano!"

Charlie jumped a little next to Emily. He turned to Emily, his face a mask of pure disbelief. A huge smile spread across his face as everyone in the room cheered. He raised his arms over his head and took a low, deep bow. Then he moved forward to collect his *second* prom king crown of the year.

As Charlie hastily made his way through the crowded ballroom toward the stage, Emily felt a little tap on her shoulder. She turned, and there was Marco, Charlie's boyfriend, standing right behind her. "Hey!" she cried, giving him a hug. "What are you doing here? Does Charlie know you're here?"

"No," Marco responded. "It's a surprise. I hit traffic coming out of Chicago, so I'm a little late. I just got here. You look great!" He grinned at Emily. They hadn't seen each other in a few months. "Where is he?"

Emily pointed to the stage, where Charlie was just ascending the steps to claim his crown. Charlie lifted his hands in the air and whooped as the crown was placed on his head. "You're dating the prom king. How does it feel?"

"Again?" Marco smiled, referring to the Memorial High prom. "I wanted to be here for him. He called me earlier this week and told me how much this prom meant to him and how sad he was that I wouldn't be here. I had no idea it meant that much to him. I've never heard Charlie be so earnest. So I e-mailed Sid and got the details. She knew I was coming, but I asked her to keep it a surprise."

"It will definitely be that," Emily said. "Hey, Marco, this is Ethan. *My* prom date." She blushed a little as she said it. Ethan shook hands with Marco and nodded knowingly. "And you remember Max, right?" Emily said, moving in closer to Ethan to make a space for Marco between her and Max.

Marco moved forward and said, "Yeah. Hey, Max. How've you been?" Max just nodded. Charlie was now leading Marisa down the stage steps toward the dance floor for their inaugural dance. Sid walked onto the stage, her guitar slung over her shoulder. She sat on a stool center stage and started to play one of Emily's favorite songs, "Hello You."

Sid sang while Charlie and Marisa danced together. Everyone had formed a big circle around the king and queen and were cheering and taking pictures. Marco excused himself and moved away from Emily, Max, and Ethan so that he was standing on the outer perimeter of the dance floor, watching Charlie from a distance. About halfway through the song, Marisa's boyfriend made his way onto the dance floor and cut in. Charlie hugged Marisa, then moved away toward the edge of the circle. The rest of the prom committee and their dates swarmed onto the dance floor and joined Marisa and her boyfriend.

Like a scene out of a movie, Charlie suddenly looked up and noticed Marco, who was now standing twenty feet away, right in Charlie's line of sight. Charlie's face broke into a huge smile. Marco moved forward, and Charlie pulled his boyfriend into a giant hug.

Ethan, who had been watching Charlie and Marco's reunion, turned to Emily and murmured, "Care to dance, gorgeous?"

"Absolutely," she declared. She looked at Max, who was standing alone next to them. "Do you mind if we dance?"

Max ran his hands through his hair. "Feel free." He gave Emily a strange, uncomfortable look that caused her stomach to flip nervously. "Actually," he said, "I'm going to take off. I have a story to finish. Tell Charlie I called a cab." And with that, he spun on his heels and walked away.

Thirteen

"Hey, Em." Max sauntered up to Emily the next Tuesday night, with Charlie in tow. Emily and Ethan were meeting the two guys to watch Sid's first gig at French's. Emily's stomach leaped at the familiar sound of her best friend's voice. She was scared to see him. *Ridiculous,* she chided herself. *This is* Max*!*

But Emily knew why she was uncomfortable—she hadn't *truly* spoken to Max since their almost moment four days earlier. They had never gone this long with awkwardness between them. They had exchanged a few lame bits of chatter on Saturday night, but she hadn't had a chance to really *talk* to him.

She was still haunted by the feelings she'd had on the boat Friday night and didn't know what to make of it. She kept trying to ignore the sensation she had felt that night, but there was something tap-tapping away in the back of her mind that just wouldn't let it go. And she had no idea if Max had felt it too.

"Hey, guys." She greeted Max and Charlie as naturally as possible. But her palm was sweaty in Ethan's hand. "Are you excited for tonight?"

Charlie beamed. "Definitely. Sid is *so* nervous." He looked giddy.

"Did Marco leave?" she asked. Emily hadn't really spoken to Charlie since Saturday night either, since she'd spent almost every spare moment with Ethan.

"Uh-huh," Charlie said, his face turning somber. "I miss him already."

"Did you guys stick around at prom for a while?" Emily asked. She and Ethan had only stayed at South's prom for a few more songs, then left to grab a bite to eat. Ethan had dropped her off at home close to midnight, and left her with a scrumptious, exhilarating good-night kiss. Thankfully everyone in her family was asleep when she got there—she was able to sneak in and hang her prom dress deep in her closet before anyone saw it and started asking questions.

Charlie nodded. "We stayed until almost the end. It's a prom king's duty." He grinned. "Then we hit the after-party at Marisa's house. I think Marco had fun. He seems to be more proprom now."

"Are you going to our prom after-party?" Max asked Emily suddenly, out of the blue. "Lauren is having an after-party at her house. I think I'm going."

Emily turned to stare at her best friend. *Lauren Ellstrom?* "Oh," she said, not sure what to say. She hadn't realized Max was going to prom, and she wondered who he was going with. How could so much happen in four days?

She realized she was being completely self-centered, but Emily didn't want Max to go to prom—she wanted to live out her own prom fantasy, but didn't want Max to have his. Totally hypocritical. "We're not sure yet what we're going to do." She looked at Ethan.

"Right," Max said distractedly. "Well, have fun." Ethan clutched Emily's hand in his, oblivious to her discomfort. Max went back to silence.

Charlie grabbed Emily's arm and pulled at her sleeve. "Can I talk to you for a sec?" he asked quietly.

She told Ethan that she'd be back in a minute, and followed Charlie toward a corner of the club. "What's up?" she asked.

"What happened between you and Max? You're acting like you hardly know each other." Charlie looked back at Ethan and Max across the room, who were standing a few feet apart without speaking.

"I don't know!" Emily exclaimed. "This is going to sound ridiculous, but I think something might have almost happened between us at Northwestern's prom—right before you showed up. It was really, really surreal."

Charlie gasped. "Like happened, happened?"

"Maybe?" Emily pushed her bangs away from her face. "I seriously don't know. But it's been weird between us ever since. I think he was really pissed at me for being late to East's prom, and now it seems like he's avoiding me, and I guess I'm sort of avoiding him because of the whole boat thing, and Ethan's fabulous and hot and perfect for me, and *I don't know!*" She sighed. "Oh, Charlie, have I massively screwed up?"

He gave her a hug. "Oh, sweetie, no. We'll figure it out." He waved at Ethan, who was shooting Emily a slightly desperate look from across the room. "What do you want to do?" he asked. "Could there be something between you and Max?"

"I might be imagining the whole thing. But I might not. Either way, I can't really get into this relationship with Ethan if I'm messing things up with my best friend, can I? I mean, Max means the world to me."

"I hate to ask this, since I sound like your mom, but"—Charlie paused—"what do you think is right? Aren't you really into Ethan?"

"Yes!"

"And what about Max?"

"I don't know. We've never gone down that road before, so I can't say for sure. I guess it's possible—there was an unfamiliar spark."

Charlie studied both guys from across the room. "You can't really go wrong with either one," he teased.

"So helpful." Emily grimaced. "I guess my biggest fear is that Ethan won't fit in with you guys. Or what if I'm imagining my chemistry with him—though I don't think I am—and I give up on Max, and then in a couple of weeks I'm left with no boyfriend and a best friend who hates me. I really need to know what Max is feeling right now. Or I need a sign that Ethan's the right guy—or that Max is."

Sid suddenly stepped onstage, guitar in hand, and the lights in the club dimmed. Charlie grabbed Emily's arm and yelled over the sound of the music, "It will work out. I promise." He pulled her back through the crowd toward the two guys waiting for them on the other side of the club.

Emily returned to Ethan's side, and he pulled her in close. Max watched them snuggle up together, then strode across the room to buy a soda. Charlie and Emily both watched him go, then shared a look.

This is bad, Emily mused silently. *And it's just going to get worse at prom.*

After the show, Emily and Ethan split off from the others. Emily had spent most of Sid's show thinking about the awkwardness between her and Max, and had finally come to a resolution about what she needed to do.

When they got to his car, Ethan pulled Emily toward him in the shadowy parking lot and ran his fingers along her cheek. She let him kiss her only briefly, then pulled away. "Can we go somewhere and talk?" she asked, walking around to her side of the car.

"Sure," Ethan said, unlocking the doors. "Everything okay?"

"I don't know," Emily responded. It was the truth. During Sid's show, Emily had realized that she needed to pursue whatever might be happening with Max. Though she felt like things with Ethan were going perfectly, she knew she could never fully enjoy their relationship if she thought it had potentially ruined things with her best friend. So she leaned back in her seat, took a deep breath, and said, "Listen, Ethan . . ."

He sighed. "You're kidding me, right?"

Am I that obvious? Emily wondered. He seemed to know where she was going, which certainly would make it easier to say. It wouldn't make it any easier for her to feel good about the decision, though. She continued, "I am having so much fun with you, but . . ."

He had started the car, but sat with the engine idling. "But?"

"But," Emily went on, "there's some stuff I need to deal with right now. I don't know how long it's going to take, or what I'm going to resolve, but I just need a little while to figure things out. I don't think it's fair to you or to me to keep hanging out." A knot crept up into her throat. She felt like sobbing as she said, "I don't think I can go to prom with you."

"So that's it?" he asked, turning toward her.

"I guess so," Emily said. "Things just don't feel right. Not right now." She knew it sounded lame, but she didn't know how else to put it. She couldn't tell him she didn't like him—that was a lie. And she couldn't say things were going nowhere—she didn't know if that was true either. She just knew something didn't feel right with her life, and she needed to try to fix it.

Ethan stared straight ahead when he repeated, "Not right now?" He turned to look at her in the darkened car. "Does that mean there's still a chance someday?"

She met his eyes in the moonlight and knew she couldn't answer his question definitively one way or the other. "I don't know. I hope so? But I know that it's not fair to hold on to you right now, and I don't expect you to wait around. I'm sorry. You have no idea how hard this is for me."

Ethan pulled out of the parking lot silently, and they rode in silence all the way to her house. Emily's hands were folded in her lap. She opened her mouth a few times to say something, but couldn't think of the right words. "I'm really sorry," she managed finally.

They pulled into the darkness outside Emily's house. Ethan hadn't parked his car in the driveway, and Emily couldn't see his expression in the darkened car. "I understand," he said, turning to look at her. "I'm sorry too. I'm really happy with you, Emily."

She choked back tears and managed to squeak out, "Me too," before she opened her door and left Ethan alone. "Good-bye, Ethan." It wasn't until she was alone in her room, tucked under her covers with her prom dress laid next to her on the bed, that Emily let herself cry.

A few nights later Emily sat alone in her bedroom again. She was picking her fingernails nervously. She felt sick.

Ethan had just called. She had offered him no further explanation, other than telling him again that she was sorry about everything and that she just couldn't commit right now. He had been understanding and kind about it, but said he was really disappointed, which had made the conversation that much harder. Emily was heartbroken; she wished they had met at a better time.

Emily had discussed the situation with Charlie and Sid at the Leaf Lounge the night before, and they had both agreed that she'd made the right decision. When Emily complained about losing Ethan, Sid had declared that Emily "needed to get over herself. Sh—crap happens." And that's how Emily felt now—like *crap*.

The phone was back in its cradle and Emily felt alone and miserable—Ethan was gone. Her dad's laptop was open on her bed in front of her, with the home page of *Buzz* on the screen. Max's prom crashing article had been published on the website a few days earlier, and Emily had finally had a chance to read it for the first time. It was really funny—he had captured all the nuances of their weeks of crashing perfectly.

He had cast Charlie, Emily, and Sid in a hilarious light, and his style was spot-on for the tone of the website. The only thing missing from the article was her and Max's maybe-almost-could-have-been-a-kiss. She wasn't surprised it wasn't in there.

Emily was so proud of Max and wanted nothing more than to tell him how excited she was for him. She knew she couldn't ignore this big achievement just because they were apparently avoiding one another. She pulled up her Instant Messenger.

E: max?
E: r you home?

Nothing. He wasn't there. Nor was he home when she called his house. She would try to find him at school the next day, but there was an assembly during their lunch period, so it was unlikely they would have any time to talk.

Sighing, she flopped off her bed and walked to her window. She had a perfect view of Max's room from her own. Emily still had the flashlight she had used as a kid to send him messages out her bedroom window, and she pulled it out from under her mattress now. She flicked it on—the light still worked.

She flipped it off and stowed it under her mattress again. Max's shade was closed, and his yard was empty. Emily couldn't believe that just a few awkward moments had put a kink in their friendship after all these years. She and Max had never even considered dating, and she wondered if maybe this was some big misunderstanding.

Until they had an honest conversation, she would just have to hope that things would go back to normal—or something better than normal. They would have to talk to each other eventually, and when they did, Emily could see if she had been alone in feeling the spark between them on the boat.

But no matter what happened with Max, one thing was certain: Emily was going to be alone for her prom.

Fourteen

"I'm not going."

Emily had told her mom that she wasn't going to prom six different ways, but her mom was still convinced maybe she would change her mind. "You'll look so pretty in navy."

"*Mom.* I'm. Not. Going. End of story."

"Maybe lavender would set off your dark hair better."

"Prom's tonight." Emily threw her hands in the air. "It's too late."

"Why aren't you going with Max?" Her mom asked the question innocently. But Emily wanted to scream and shout and tell her she was horrible for asking such a loaded question.

Why aren't I going with Max? she fretted as she stomped up the stairs to her room. She had obviously been debating this very question for the past few days and couldn't come up with an answer she was happy with—other than the fact that he was going with someone else, of course.

"Are you okay, Emily?" Abby's pigtailed head poked around the door of Emily's room, breaking her out of her head.

"Yeah. Fine."

"Do you want me to go to prom with you?" Abby looked so sincere that Emily knew she hadn't asked the question to be malicious or to make Emily feel totally lame. Abby just wanted Emily to be happy.

"Come here," Emily beckoned, and her sister happily trotted into the room and curled up next to Emily on her bed. "Thank you for offering to be my prom date."

Abby grinned and snuggled into her sister's arm. "You're welcome."

"You know what?" Emily closed her eyes. "I've been really stupid for the past couple of months."

"Stupid how?"

"I guess I thought that prom with my best friend would somehow be less perfect

214

than prom with a knight in shining armor, who would buy me a pretty rose corsage and kiss me at the end of the night. And now that misguided fantasy made me lose my best friend."

"Do you like roses?" Abby was missing the point, but Emily was relieved. Her sister didn't need to worry about stuff like this yet. She'd get her share of it someday.

"Yeah, roses are pretty. But Max would have probably brought me a daisy corsage or something silly and frivolous, just to be different." Emily paused. "And I would have loved it." She sighed, and Abby snuggled in deeper. "But you know what?" She asked that question blankly, quietly, more to herself than to her sister. "Prom with Ethan would have been perfect too. He would have more than definitely kissed me next to the buffet table and made all my prom fantasies come true."

Abby craned her neck around to study Emily's face. "Is there a buffet at prom? Do they have mini hot dogs?"

"But if I'd gone with Ethan . . ." Emily ignored her sister's question and continued her musings. Abby was like a free therapy session. Her questions were unrelated to the point of the conversation, but there was something soothing about having her there. It was making Emily think about things in a way she normally wouldn't. " . . . I would always wonder if the connection between me and Max was real or imagined."

As she said it, Emily knew she had to find out more. Her friendship with Max was built on too much to have it ruined by the uncertainty of not knowing what *might* have happened. That's why she'd broken up with Ethan, after all. It's the reason she'd given up her chance for a perfect prom. She couldn't face looking back at prom as the night that caused her friendship with Max to end. No amount of romance was worth that.

So if she was doing the right thing, how was everything still so totally wrong?

"What am I doing?" Emily asked no one in particular.

"You were going to get me a snack?" Charlie offered helpfully.

"Why am I missing my own prom?"

"Because you broke up with your yummy new boyfriend, didn't want to go with me, and completely screwed things up with your backup-date-slash-best-friend-slash-maybe-future-loooover." Charlie smiled. "Does that answer the question?"

Emily groaned. She was curled up on the couch in her family room, with Charlie's feet partially blocking her view of the TV (she didn't mind—she wasn't watching anyway). *Pretty in Pink* was on, in honor of the fact that Emily had screwed up her prom night and now wanted to watch Molly Ringwald get all dolled up and live out her happy ending.

Charlie had offered to take Emily to prom, but she refused to be the girl who went with her cousin. She really believed that might be worse than not going at all.

"You could have gone with me," Sid chimed in. She was stretched out on the floor, facedown.

"I should have." Emily smiled. "At least I would have gotten points for going with a rock star. I could have said I knew you when."

Sid blushed. She still hadn't gotten used to the fact that she was now a *real* rock star. After her gig at French's earlier that week, 1492 had been so impressed with her performance and the crowd's reaction that they had offered her a spot touring with their band when they hit the road in a couple of months. "Aw, shucks," she said. "You make it sound like I've already turned into a diva. Give me time, lurves, give me time." She looked up and grinned. Her now-green hair streak flopped over one eye.

"I'm going to go put on my dress," Emily announced suddenly. "I can pretend I'm going to a John Hughes prom with Andrew McCarthy."

"Oh, Em." Charlie sighed. "Don't do it. That's just sad."

Emily laughed. "No, really, I think it will help. Yes, it *sounds* sad, but *I* believe that wearing my dress will make me feel *better*." Charlie and Sid looked at each other with wide eyes.

"Girl, you're nuts." Sid's voice was muffled by the carpet.

Emily laughed and bounded up the stairs to her room and closed the door. Her parents had gone out for the night—taking Abby with them—so she knew she would probably be left alone. But she shut the door just in case. She wanted a few minutes to herself.

Opening her closet, Emily pulled her

prom dress from the back corner and laid it out on her bed. She sat next to it, staring out across her backyard through the window—fireflies flickered periodically in the dusky sky, like mini Christmas tree lights.

After a few minutes of staring without really seeing, Emily realized a light besides the one coming from her own bedroom was shining into her backyard as well. Max's bedroom light was on. Emily checked her alarm clock. Prom had started an hour ago, so he shouldn't still be home.

Then Emily noticed someone moving in Max's room, and she recognized her best friend's striped oxford. *Why isn't he at prom?* she wondered. Suddenly Max turned and looked out the window. He spotted Emily looking at him from her window. They stared at each other without movement for a few moments.

Emily backed away from her window, turning off her light. Reaching under her mattress, she grabbed the flashlight she had discovered a few days earlier and shined it at Max's window. A few seconds later Max's light flicked off and he flash-lighted her back. Emily smiled in her darkened room.

She needed to talk to him immediately. She couldn't handle one more second of not knowing what was going on between them. Leaving her flashlight in the on position, propped up on her windowsill facing Max's room, she turned and jogged back down the stairs.

As she thumped out the front door, Emily could hear Charlie calling after her. She heard footsteps following her but didn't care. She just needed to talk to Max. She ran around the corner of her house and into Max's backyard. There was an old oak tree that Emily had climbed a million times—just not for a few years. She awkwardly ascended it now, carefully avoiding the thin, brittle branch halfway up the tree.

Charlie and Sid were beneath her now, calling out in hushed yells. "What are you doing?" Charlie asked. "Em, come down."

Emily shook her head, though she knew Charlie couldn't see her in the dim light. "I have to talk to Max," she replied, huffing from the effort of climbing the tree. "Don't worry—I've done this a million times." She reached Max's room and tap-tap-tapped on the window from her perch in the tree.

Max's bedroom light flashed on, illuminating Emily in the tree. She was sure she looked ridiculous. "What the . . ." Max was just as surprised to see Emily as Emily was to realize she'd just climbed the tree.

"Hey," she panted. "How are you?"

"Okay." He crossed his arms over his chest. "What are you doing here? Shouldn't you be at prom?"

"Shouldn't you?"

"No." Max looked down. "I don't have a date."

"I thought you were going with Lauren Ellstrom?"

"I never said that."

"You did. We were talking about the prom after-party, and you said you were going with Lauren."

"No." Max shook his head. "I said I was going to Lauren's after-party. But I never said anything about going to prom with Lauren."

"But you . . ." Emily stopped. This was going nowhere. "Max, listen." She paused. She still hadn't really thought out how she was going to approach this awkward subject. "I'm really sorry about being late to meet you last weekend."

"That's okay," he replied. "The story got written."

Emily was sidetracked for a second. "I know! It was so good—I read it and am so impressed."

"Thanks." He looked at her expectantly.

"But, um—okay, listen." Emily settled into a more comfortable position in the branch of the tree. "I've been feeling really weird lately about something. I don't know how to bring this up, but I sort of feel like we have to talk about it or I'm just never going to know if I was imagining something or—"

Max cut her off. "I was a little freaked about what almost happened on the boat too."

"You were?!" She wondered if she should be worried about his choice of words— "freaked" wasn't exactly reassuring. She continued. "Did you feel like there was almost a moment?"

"Yeah," Max answered sheepishly. "But then Charlie showed up and you found Ethan and everything got . . ."

"Weird." They said it at the same time, then laughed.

Emily spoke first. "I broke things off with Ethan." Her heart pitter-pattered when she said that.

"He seemed like a good guy."

"Yeah," Emily agreed. "He is. But what I had with him isn't as important as what I have with you."

There was a pause. Max was looking at her in the moonlight. *Is he going to kiss me?* she wondered. Her heart thumped in her chest.

And then Max started laughing. Not just a little laugh, either. It was a big, from-the-gut, almost-falling-out-the-window guffaw. Emily had just bared her soul—if she was using romance writer language—and Max was *laughing*.

She stared at him for a moment, then she too started laughing. Tears pooled in the corners of her eyes, and the branch she sat on was shaking.

Max's dimples deepened. "It's so great to hear you say that. . . . I'm sorry, I don't mean to laugh."

"No, I get it," she said, matching his smile. "This feels better, doesn't it?" Emily asked. She knew Max was feeling exactly the same way she was. There was absolutely nothing romantic between them. There never would be.

"Much," Max confessed. "Don't get me wrong—there was some sort of spark the other night, and maybe there's been some funky spark sparking around for the past month—but I think we were both just caught up in a bizarre, promesque mood." Some friendships were meant to be just that—friendships—and hers and Max's was one of those. He reached out and touched her hand. "We're much better off as best friends, aren't we?"

Emily nodded. "Agreed." Then she leaned forward on her branch to give him a hug. It was awkward, considering that she was balanced somewhat precariously in the oak tree, but it still felt good. "But you know what?" she said, suddenly remembering her prom dress draped across her bed next door. "I wouldn't want to go to prom with anyone but you. We really should have planned to go together."

"I offered," Max declared. "You shot me down!"

"I know, I know." Emily groaned. "Okay, I'll admit that I would have really liked to have my romantic prom fantasy come true. But now I'm thinking a little excitement and intrigue on prom night is way more fun than a lot of romance."

"I agree."

"And could Ethan—however yummy he

is—live up to the standards you, Charlie, and Sid have set for prom? I think not. Kissing by the buffet table just doesn't compare to the excitement of prom crashing." She paused and looked down at Charlie and Sid, who were still standing, looking up at her from the base of the tree. "So," she said, loud enough for the other two to hear, "who wants to go to Humphrey's prom?"

"Em," Max said slowly. "None of us have tickets, remember?"

"Ah," Emily said. "That hasn't stopped us before, has it?"

Max's dimples deepened again. Charlie started clapping from his post on the ground. "One more target?" he asked excitedly.

Emily grinned. "That's what I'm thinking."

Emily heard her parents' car pull into the driveway just as she emerged from her room in her perfect pink prom dress a few minutes later. By the time she got to the top of the stairs, Abby was clapping with Charlie and Sid in the front hall as Emily's mom snapped pictures of her elder daughter descending the stairs. Her mom was so caught up in the excitement of it all that she didn't seem to notice that Emily had a prom dress she knew nothing about and had never seen before. Emily was sure the questions would come later.

When Max walked through the Bronsons' front door decked out in his tux a few minutes later, Emily's mom couldn't stop herself from tearing up. With the camera following his every move, Max happily wrapped his arm around Emily's waist and together they posed for pictures with huge grins on their faces. Emily's mom only let them go when she was certain she had at least one shot that would be good enough for the Bronson family Christmas newsletter.

It was after ten o' clock by the time they finally arrived at Humphrey's prom. They had swung by Charlie's and Sid's houses to pick up their formal wear too, then all of them put last-minute touches on their hair and outfits in the car outside the convention center. Charlie was still trying to tie his bow tie as they rode the escalator up to the ballroom that had been the site of Max and Emily's first prom together—Park High— just four weeks earlier. Emily couldn't believe how much had happened since.

"Hello, Emily." Mrs. Fenton, Humphrey's composition teacher, greeted her at the door of the ballroom. She was checking people in and collecting their tickets. "Max, how are you?"

"Hi, Mrs. Fenton," Emily responded politely.

"How's your mom?" Mrs. Fenton gave Emily a knowing smile. It was the same smile all the teachers gave her. The one that said, *I know a lot more about you than you would ever guess, because your mom talks about your private life in the teachers' lounge, but I'm going to pretend I don't know that you still grind your teeth in the night, et cetera.* Emily hated that smile. "She must be so excited about you going to prom."

What she didn't say is, *I know she was worried about how you were a huge loser who didn't get a date for prom, so isn't this exciting that things worked out for you?* At least, that's what Emily was imagining she was thinking in her head.

"My mom is fine. She got lots of pictures." Emily smiled back. "Have a good night, Mrs. Fenton. Enjoy prom!" She started to walk through the door, with Charlie, Max, and Sid trailing close on her heels.

They were steps away from the door of the ballroom when Mrs. Fenton called out. "Oh, Emily!" Emily turned back, a nervous smile plastered on her mouth. "I need to take your tickets."

"Oh," Emily said, thinking quickly. "We turned them in earlier tonight when we first got here. We just stepped outside for a quick breath of fresh air. But we're back now!" She sounded way too chipper.

"That's impossible," Mrs. Fenton said. "We have a lockdown policy, so if you leave, you leave for good. No readmittance. You understand, right, dear?" Mrs. Fenton suddenly looked like a mean old lady.

"Of course." Emily sugarcoated her response. She could tell Charlie and Max were both laughing silently behind her. "Well, good night then."

They turned and rode the escalator back down to the lower level of the convention center. Rejected.

"Plan B?" Charlie jumped off the last step of the escalator.

"Looks that way," Max responded. "Very suave, Em. Nice attempt."

Emily shrugged. "It was worth a shot, right? Now I guess we have to get in the hard way."

"Breaking and entering?" Sid asked hopefully. "I noticed a side door that looked pretty unguarded up there."

They all agreed and moved to the east

entrance of the convention center. They climbed a set of stairs to the ballroom level. There was a catering service door that led into the kitchen. Sid stood cover as the other three slid along a wall and ducked through the door, then she followed.

The kitchen was steamy and loud, with waiters and busboys bustling through the crowded mazelike countertops. The four of them weaved through the kitchen, following a team of waiters carrying trays of hors d'oeuvres out into the ballroom. The door swung open to reveal Humphrey's prom in full swing.

"Easy peasy!" Charlie declared, moving into the ballroom while straightening his jacket. "Let's get down!"

Charlie and Max grabbed Sid—despite her protests—and pulled her onto the dance floor. Emily was dispatched to grab sodas.

She noticed a few of her old swimming friends across the room and waved. They waved back, and Emily realized why her own prom meant more to her than the other proms they'd crashed. The whole room was full of friends. These were the people she had spent the past four years with—and some she'd known as long as thirteen years, if you counted those who'd gone to the same elementary school.

She really *was* going to miss the comforts and familiarity of home next year. Suddenly nostalgic, she looked back at the dance floor to find Max, Charlie, and Sid. Charlie and Sid were rocking out in the middle of the dance floor, while Max chatted with Lauren Ellstrom nearby. He looked really happy—Emily was happy *for* him.

Waiting for her sodas at the bar, Emily looked around the ballroom at all the couples and friends dancing and laughing in their dresses and tuxes. Even though her prom had a familiar, friendly feel, Emily still felt something was missing. She'd had a riot crashing proms with her friends—it had been the perfect ending to high school, and the perfect cure for senior slide. She knew she would have always regretted it if she'd gone to her prom with Ethan and jeopardized her and Max's friendship . . . but she missed Ethan horribly. He'd been so perfect for her.

She hustled over to the dance floor and joined her friends. The song that had been playing ended, and the DJ kicked off the next song—Green Day's "Good Riddance (Time of Your Life)"—with a dedication.

"This next song goes out to Emily . . . who finally made it to the right prom."

Charlie gasped and both Max and Sid looked at Emily. "I didn't dedicate this song to you!" Charlie declared.

"Not me," Max shrugged.

Sid sighed. "Are you kidding?"

Charlie lowered his voice to a hushed whisper. "Who knows about us?"

They all looked around, searching for the person who had uncovered their plot. Emily's stomach fluttered nervously—she was totally busted. It was their last prom, and she'd been caught by someone.

The lights on the dance floor dimmed, and a figure stepped out from behind the DJ booth and onto the dance floor. Emily turned just as Max, Charlie, and Sid all noticed that the person was winding through the crowded dance floor toward them.

Emily's breath caught in her throat—it was Ethan. "Good dedication?" he asked, trying to hide a smile. But his eyes gave him away—Emily could tell he was about to laugh. "You look nervous."

"Was that your dedication? How did you . . . ? What are you . . . ?" Emily stuttered. "Are you a DJ?"

Ethan laughed. "No, I'm not a DJ. But my cousin is—with a little help from him, I was able to crash your prom. I owed you, right?" He looked unbelievably proud.

Max nudged Sid and Charlie, suggesting that maybe they should take off and give Emily and Ethan some alone time. Both Sid and Charlie nudged him back and stayed put. They wanted to know where this was going.

"Oh," Emily said lamely.

Ethan looked suddenly uncomfortable and glanced around, as if searching for someone. "You're here with someone, aren't you?"

"What?" Emily asked. When she realized he was asking if she had a date, she laughed. "Oh! No." Then she saw Charlie, Sid, and Max all grinning at her goofily from a polite distance away. "Well, actually, I'm with my friends. But they're great dates, and they're willing to share, if that's what you're asking."

"I wanted to see you, Emily." Ethan suddenly turned serious. "When we had our conversation earlier this week, I didn't know what to say. But the more I thought about it, the more I realized how wrong you were. We're good together. We need to give this thing a shot. I'm hoping you might be ready now."

Emily smiled and twirled her hair. "So you crashed my prom to find me?"

"I figured it was the only way to show you I meant it. I was hoping you'd show up. I assumed you wouldn't miss it."

"You were right," she agreed. "And you're right about us, too. Thank you for giving me time to figure things out."

Ethan held out his hand. "Dance with me?"

Charlie, Sid, and Max all whistled. They were totally unsubtle, but Emily would have expected no less. Ethan bowed in response, earning him an extra cheer from Charlie.

She let him pull her close and rested her chin on Ethan's shoulder. They had drifted to one side of the dance floor, away from the crowds of other dancers.

As the song ended, Ethan pulled back slightly and turned Emily's face toward his. She smiled at him, and he kissed her. Emily let the rest of the room blur out of focus— she could only see Ethan and a tray of tiny sandwiches over his left shoulder.

Melting into his next kiss, Emily sighed happily. She was being kissed next to the buffet table at prom. Some dreams do come true.

About the Author

Erin (Soderberg) Downing has been to six high school formals, two of them proms. She has worn green, white, sparkly, and black dresses . . . but never pink. Like Danny, she always sort of wanted to go in a silly costume, but never had the nerve. In the process of writing this book, she did not crash any proms—and in fact has never crashed anything in her life. A native of Duluth, Minnesota, Erin currently resides outside New York City with her husband and daughter. She is also the author of the Simon Pulse Romantic Comedy *Dancing Queen*. Visit her on the Web at www.erindowning.com

LOL at this sneak peek of

Gettin' Lucky

By Micol Ostow

A new Romantic Comedy from Simon Pulse

TOP FIVE EXOTIC, COOL LOCATIONS TO SPEND NEW YEAR'S EVE
*(in no particular order)

1. A private capsule on the London Eye.
2. The top of the Eiffel Tower (clichéd, especially ever since a *certain* movie star went and ruined it for the rest of us, but still).
3. Backstage at a Killers show with the cast of *The O.C.*
4. A chalet tucked into the highest corners of the Swiss Alps.
5. Zip-lining along the Costa Rican jungle canopy.

(For all of the above scenarios, one should assume a romantic interest in tow.)

Note that nowhere on this list is Spring Brook, New Jersey. This is because Spring Brook, New Jersey, is not an especially cool place to spend New Year's Eve. Particularly if it is the home of one's grandparents, median age seventy-two. Double-particularly if one's boyfriend is spending the holiday in Aspen, with his hotshot ski-patrolling friends.

Not that I'm bitter or anything.

Normally I wouldn't mind. My grandparents are totally sweet, and I actually really like spending time with them. But it's definitely an unwritten rule in the teenage handbook that not getting kissed at midnight on New Year's Eve is like a karmic slap in the face. Or, if it's not, it should be. It's in *my* handbook, anyway. I mean, the midnight kiss is the launchpad of a happy and prosperous twelve months, and smooching my grandfather on the cheek rather than my superhot boyfriend on the smacker just seemed like I was *asking* for trouble, karmically speaking.

But I digress. I made the best of it, laughing along gamely to Ryan Seacrest and sipping at sparkling apple cider. Jesse texted me at exactly midnight, which I thought was extremely romantic, even if it wasn't quite the same thing as real-time kissage. We did the best we could.

Now, though, I could hardly wait to see him. So much so that I'd traded in my direct flight from Newark International for a rockin' three-hour layover in Houston, Texas, just so I could make it home a full twenty-four hours earlier than expected.

It was all part of my grand plan.

Jesse had been home, back in Vegas, for a full two days while I withered away in Central Jersey on a steady diet of PBS, classical music, and Kashi, the three absolutes of my grandparents' household. Jesse expected me to get in tomorrow, the day before school started.

But I was coming in *today*.

I was coming in today, and I was going to see Jesse. Never mind that I'd spent a glassy-eyed three hours wandering the Houston duty-free and robotically stuffing my face with sour gummy bears. Never mind that my face had a fine sheen of airplane scum settling across its surface. Never mind that my hair—washed and styled so impeccably first thing this morning, back in Spring Brook—had wilted worse than the cheeseburgers that I found at the airport food court. In my mind's eye, I somehow still managed to look like a supermodel. (My mind's eye is really forgiving.) And I was totally going to surprise Jesse.

Thankfully, all of my flights were on time and I made my connection and didn't lose my luggage or any of those annoying things that can happen when you travel. The oily skin and weird, limp hair was sort of the worst of it. My father was waiting at the airport when I got off the plane—he'd made up a sign for me in bright green Sharpie that said CASSANDRA ELISE PARKER, playing at being a fancy driver or something—and was in on all of my machinations.

He hugged me and grabbed my suitcase away from me, saying, "You look thin, Cass. Did you eat in New Jersey?"

Do you see why I adore my father?

I nodded. "I did, actually. A lot." Kind of too much. Pigging out on Kashi is not recommended.

He smiled. "Grandma and Grandpa are pretty serious about their three squares."

"Right?" I said, laughing.

He led me out to the parking lot, where we spent about twenty minutes trying to figure out where he had parked. Then on the drive back home he wanted to know about my trip.

"It was fun," I said, mostly meaning it.

You know, not "Aspen-with-your-boyfriend" fun, but fun.

"But you can't wait to see Jesse," Dad said, filling in the blanks.

I nodded. "That's why I'm here," I said, even though he already knew that.

"Well"—he checked his watch—"we should be home in fifteen minutes. If you can get to Jesse by four, do you think you can be done surprising him and back home by six? I know it doesn't give you a lot of time, but I have to be at the restaurant for the dinner rush."

How could I say no? Dad wasn't even implying anything gross by his use of the phrase "surprising him." At least, I hope he wasn't. And, anyway, we could always use Jesse's car if we wanted to go out later on.

"Of course," I said, sighing with satisfaction. I leaned back in my seat and went into a slow, trancelike state of Zen. I watched the scenery change through the blur of my window, from airport-related industrial waste to rocky, red-tinged mountains. Soon the glitter of the Strip would be upon us, and I would be home. My dog, a mangy and borderline insane Boston terrier named Maxine, would be waiting for me.

And so would Jesse.

Jesse only lives about five minutes from me, mainly because all of us who don't live in the city proper (which is most of us) live in the same three-mile radius of surrounding suburbs. And, while living just outside of Vegas, a.k.a. Sin City, might seem really edgy and exotic, it sort of only affects us in really peripheral ways. Sure, there are the occasional out-there dates where we go off to pose with Indiana Jones and Britney Spears at the wax museum, or gondola rides at the Venetian. And yes, if we go out to celebrate at a fancy dinner, there is an 80 percent chance that we'll catch a glimpse of a certain blond celebutante with a reputation for dancing on tables. Kids here learn to play online poker long before they've even been given their first PlayStation (you don't even have to bet money, thank goodness). But really, it's not so scandalous. Mostly we all live very regular lives.

Jesse's house, for instance, is a completely normal, completely modest split-level, trimmed in aluminum siding and boasting a totally misleading BEWARE OF DOG sign on the front square of lawn. Jesse's mother has a froufy little white dog that would inspire terror in no one. But I suppose the sign is just for effect. Not that Maxine is all that hardcore, but I really can't get down with dogs small enough to fit in a pocketbook. Don't tell Jesse's mom, though. For now, at least, she likes me.

I pulled up smoothly, humming to the radio, parked, and killed the ignition. Jesse's car, a Civic adorned with stickers from all of his various athletic affiliations, sat in the driveway, so at least I knew he was home. This was good. My surprise really would have had much less of an impact if he'd been out, obviously.

I tapped my lucky rabbit foot that Dad had kindly allowed me to hang from the rearview mirror and briefly crossed my fingers. Even though Jesse and I had been together for about a year now, I still got a little bit fluttery when I hadn't seen him in a while. And I think the element of surprise was upping my nerves, too. I jumped out of the car and made my way up the front walk, taking a moment to smooth my hair down. It was looking slightly perkier now that I was back in the desert climes of Vegas. New Jersey humidity and I do *not* get along.

I rang the doorbell and tried to look nonchalant as I waited for someone to answer the door. In my mind, Jesse pulled the door open, erupted into a thousand-watt grin at the sight of me, and swooped me up in his arms, finally dipping me gracefully into a flawless Hollywood kiss.

In point of fact, what actually happened was that Jesse's younger brother, Paul, opened the door and scowled at me. Paul was twelve, which put him at prime sulking age.

"Hi!" I said brightly, trying to ignore the fact that he didn't seem to care one way or another about my arrival. "I came home early!"

He managed an all-but-imperceptible nod. "Okay. Jesse's upstairs. Our mom's not home," he added as an afterthought, smirking. He really was rushing into the adolescence thing full-force.

Despite the fact that I wanted to go charging up the stairs at top speed, I forced myself to walk like a normal, non-crazy, non-boyfriend-starved person. When I got to Jesse's bedroom door, I paused and took a deep breath. My heart was going crazy. Which later on I would look back on as some sort of omen or whatever, but really was probably much more straightforward and meaningless. I mean, how could I have known?

Music was blaring out of Jesse's room—Kelly Clarkson, which would ensure no small amount of teasing once our reunion kissing was out of the way. I giggled, rapped hard on the door, and called out.

"Surprise!" I shouted, gleeful.

I grabbed his doorknob.

I turned it.

I pushed.

And gasped.

Jesse did not seem to have heard me knock at his door, or call out to him. He did not notice that his bedroom door had opened and that I was now standing in his doorway. He was completely oblivious to my presence, for better or for worse.

For better, because I'd like to think that if he'd known that I was standing there, he might have ceased and desisted all suspicious activity.

For worse, because said suspicious activity seemed to involve swallowing my best friend's face whole.

The blood drained from my face and I felt faint. There, right before my plane-puffy and red-rimmed eyes, were Jesse and Alana. Kissing. And possibly doing some other stuff that was maybe a little more PG-13. His hand was buried in her straight-ironed, low-lighted, meticulously layered hair. Her premium-denim-clad legs were splayed across his legs. Kelly Clarkson sounded incredibly chipper about this whole state of affairs.

I, however, wanted to die.

"What the . . . ?" I started, grabbing against the door frame to keep myself steady.

Fortunately, just then Kelly stopped wailing, and Jesse and Alana were finally aware of my presence. They had the good grace, at least, to spring apart to opposite sides of the bed guiltily, Alana furtively straightening out the hem of her tank top. She wiped at her mouth with the back of her hand, silent.

A power guitar chord cut through the tension, and I nearly jumped out of my skin. Sheepishly, Jesse grabbed at a remote and shut the stereo down. Now you could hear a pin drop again. That, or the tiny, tearing sound of my heart as it made its way through the meat grinder that was my best friend and boyfriend's betrayal.

Ouch.

The awkwardness threatened to suffocate us. Finally Jesse cleared his throat, breaking the silence. He ran his fingers through his unruly brown hair.

"So," he started, looking equal parts embarrassed, ashamed, and confused. "You're home early."

Get smitten with these sweet & sassy British treats:

**Gucci Girls
by Jasmine Oliver**

Three friends tackle the high-stakes world of fashion school.

**10 Ways to Cope with Boys
by Caroline Plaisted**

What every girl *really* needs to know.

**Ella Mental
by Amber Deckers**

If only every girl had a "Good Sense" guide!

From Simon Pulse · Published by Simon & Schuster